it has not kindness in its spirit, nor mercy in its mind

it snorted and stamped its feet on the shingle shore

With a tremendous judder the ship struck hard, and stuck fast.

not the footprints of a man nor woman

bind your promise with a kiss

deep dark waters of Loch Ness

Theresa Breslin

Theresa Breslin is a highly acclaimed,
Carnegie Medal-winning author, who has published
over forty books for children and young adults. She lives
near Glasgow, Scotland. Her work has been filmed for
television, adapted for stage and radio, and translated into
many languages. Theresa worked as a librarian before
becoming a full-time writer; she is passionate about
children's literature and literacy.

Kate Leiper

Kate Leiper is an artist and illustrator
based in Edinburgh, Scotland. She studied at Gray's
School of Art in Aberdeen, and her work has been exhibited in
galleries from London to the north of Scotland. She has been
commissioned for projects by the Scottish Storytelling Centre
and the Royal Lyceum Theatre. Inspirations for her work
range from Scottish folklore, to tales from
the Far East, to Shakespeare.

the everlasting snow that rests there

The sky darkened as an enormous winged Beast with hooked talons, glittering eyes

An Illustrated Treasury of

Scottish Mythical Creatures

Theresa Breslin

Kate Leiper

Floris
Books

A magic door in the rocks crashed open

This book is for

Seán Harris Houston – T.B.
Lesley and Malcolm – K.L.

when the moon rises but the sun hardly sets

the seals came ashore and danced

First published in 2015 by Floris Books. Fourth printing 2019
Text © Theresa Breslin 2015. Illustrations © Kate Leiper 2015
Theresa Breslin and Kate Leiper have asserted their right
under the Copyright, Designs and Patent Act 1988
to be identified as the Author and Illustrator of this Work
www.florisbooks.co.uk
British Library CIP data available. ISBN 978–178250–195–4
Printed in Poland through Hussar

Contents

deep dark waters of Loch Ness

something he had never seen before

The wind strengthened

hail beat in his face

The Monster of Loch Ness

Loch Ness is an ideal place for a monster. It is so deep that it has more water in it than all the lakes of England and Wales added together – so who knows what might be lurking in a cave far below the surface?

There is a record of a massive beast terrorising the folk who lived near Loch Ness when St Columba of Iona was visiting the area. The people there, who spoke Gaelic, named it Niseag, which became 'Nessie' in English – the name by which our monster is now known all over the world.

In the days when monsters
roamed the earth,

they kept mainly to high mountains, deep waters or far islands.

The monsters were big and scary-looking and knew that when they wandered near the homes of human folk they caused terror and alarm. Humans usually shrieked and ran into their houses when they saw a monster. But from time to time they armed themselves with swords and sticks and stones to chase one. If they caught it,

they would keep it in a cage or even kill it. So the monsters learned to stay in remote places and went about their business unobtrusively – sometimes living right under the noses of human folk without being noticed.

Nowadays, monsters still keep themselves well hidden, but if you search carefully, you will find out where they are.

If you mull over a map of Scotland you will see their outlines on the islands.

If you scan the Scottish mountains you will see their shapes where they lie sleeping.

And if you watch the deep dark waters of Loch Ness for long enough, you will see the monster who dwells there.

In Olden Times, the people who lived by the shores of Loch Ness were farm folk, fisher folk and ferry folk. On the green land surrounding the loch, the farm folk tended their cattle and crops. In the waters of the loch, the fisher folk spread their nets and caught fish. Up and down and across the loch from side to side, between hamlets and harbours, the ferry folk plied their boats to carry passengers and goods and livestock.

Among these ferry folk was a boy named 'McKenzie'. McKenzie's father had been a ferryman and so had his father before him, and so had *his* father before *him*, and so on and so on, as far back as anyone could remember. His ferryboat journeyed from the

furthest southwestern point of the loch at the entrance to the Great Glen, downstream to the furthest northeastern point at the port of Inverness. McKenzie was very familiar with the waters of Loch Ness. He knew the safest route to avoid the patches of weed and reed that might tangle on the rudder of his boat. With his hand on the tiller, he was adept at steering his way through the swirls and eddies of the loch in good weather and in bad. In good weather the loch was beautiful to behold and peaceful to sail upon. In bad weather the loch could be extremely dangerous, for there is more water in Loch Ness than there is in every loch and lake in England and Wales added together. An unexpected flurry of wind could make the waves choppy and rock the ferryboat violently.

One winter – the worst for many years – crops failed, cattle died, and in the loch the fishing was poor. Each home suffered for lack of food.

On a bleak midday McKenzie had moored his boat and was preparing to eat his dinner of two small fish and a handful of oatmeal when he sensed that he was being watched. He looked up. A grey head bobbed in the water nearby. Two eyes gazed at his fish. It was too large to be an otter but it was strange for a seal to be so far inland. McKenzie thought that perhaps starvation had driven the animal here. It certainly seemed hungry. He glanced at his two fish. This was a meagre meal for him, but he did have the oatmeal too. He lifted the two fish and threw them over the side of his boat. The creature opened its mouth to catch them. Only as its head came out of the water did McKenzie realise the extent of its neck. He leapt to his feet and stared in disbelief. This was no seal. It was something he had never seen before. The animal's neck was the length of his boat! Where it joined the body there was an enormous hump and, after that, an even *longer* tail. McKenzie gaped as the monster towered above him. A single flick of its tail could smash his boat to pieces. But the monster dipped its head as if saying 'thank you'. Making wide ripples, it dived under the surface of the loch and the waters became quiet again.

McKenzie resolved not to mention the monster to anyone. Folk did gossip about seeing monsters but few believed these stories. If he told of what he had seen, people might laugh at him. Or, if they thought his tale was true, they might hunt the monster – out of fear or for food. They definitely wouldn't be happy with what he was doing, which was dropping some fish into the water whenever he passed that spot in the loch.

Later that same winter, McKenzie was on his route to Inverness one evening when a storm blew up. The wind strengthened, and hail beat in his face. He had no passengers on board, and he was glad of that, for the boat was heaving as the heavy current dragged it along. Using all his strength McKenzie grasped the tiller to guide his boat. If he didn't deliver his cargo of barrels and boxes to Inverness he would not be paid. The waves grew stronger and pounded against the hull as he tried to hold his boat on a steady course. Then a freakish gust struck. The boat spun out of control, and with a horrible grinding tearing noise, the rudder broke off!

Now there was no means of steering. McKenzie was at the mercy of the wind and the waves. His boat was pulled this way and that by the force of the storm. The boxes and barrels began to roll and slide around. McKenzie grabbed a box and hauled it back into the centre of the deck. But it was no good. As soon as he put one box in place, another slipped loose. Water was swilling into the boat. Within minutes it would be swamped. The boat would tip over and McKenzie would end up in the freezing cold waters of the loch.

Suddenly there was a hard dunt at the stern and the whole boat shuddered.

"Ah, no!" McKenzie cried. "I have hit a rock!"

He peered over the side. A round grey lump was sticking out of the water. McKenzie groaned. If the rock had torn a hole below the waterline his boat would sink in seconds. In the gloom he saw the grey lump rise up from the waves, and two eyes looked into his. It was not a rock. It was the monster!

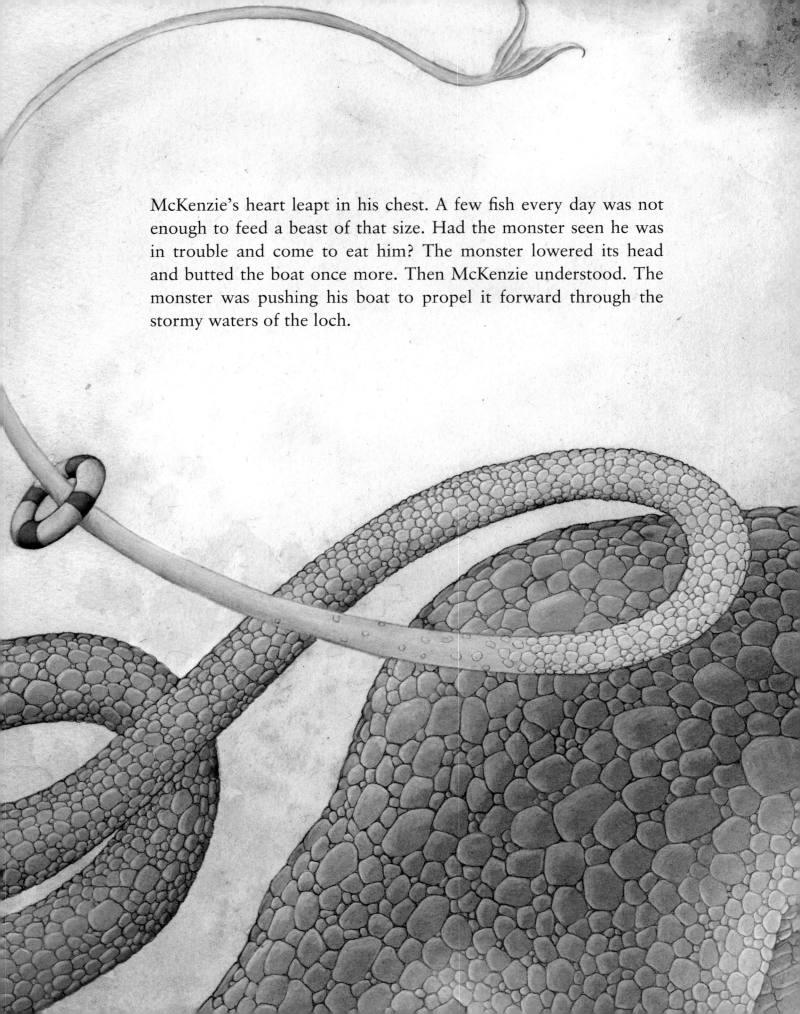

McKenzie's heart leapt in his chest. A few fish every day was not enough to feed a beast of that size. Had the monster seen he was in trouble and come to eat him? The monster lowered its head and butted the boat once more. Then McKenzie understood. The monster was pushing his boat to propel it forward through the stormy waters of the loch.

It was almost daylight when McKenzie reached Inverness. The banks of the loch were crowded with people, for the ferry folk are like family and they had come to search for him. Their lanterns shone out in the darkness and they carried poles with long hooks at the end to grapple the boat and draw it safe to the pier.

As they did so, the monster raised its head from the water. McKenzie waved his thanks as it swam away. But from the shore came screams and shouts.

"A wild beast!"

"It has come to attack us!"

"It will eat our children!"

"Kill the monster! Kill the monster!"

Quickly McKenzie tied up his boat. Men and women were running hither and thither, calling to each other.

"Bring swords!"

"Bring sticks!"

"Bring stones!"

"We must arm ourselves and hunt the monster down."

"No!" McKenzie tried to calm them. "This monster is a kindly beast."

"There is no such thing as a kind monster," they told him. "We must kill it before it harms us."

"This monster means no harm," McKenzie pleaded. But nothing he said could change their minds.

"The monster was chasing you," they told him.

"The monster was helping me," McKenzie replied.

"The monster will eat our children," they told him.

"The monster eats only fish," McKenzie replied.

"How do you know this?" one man asked suspiciously. "Are you a friend of this monster?"

McKenzie saw that he could say nothing more or they would turn their fear and anger on him and he too would be in danger.

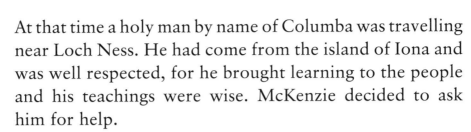

At that time a holy man by name of Columba was travelling near Loch Ness. He had come from the island of Iona and was well respected, for he brought learning to the people and his teachings were wise. McKenzie decided to ask him for help.

Columba of Iona listened to McKenzie's story. He went to the water's edge where the people had gathered to begin their hunt for the monster. A hazel tree was growing there, and from it he cut wood to make himself a long staff. Then Columba stretched out his arm so that the hazel staff lay over the waters of Loch Ness and he said aloud:

"O, monster of the loch, I bid you to appear before me."

All present looked at the loch, but the waters remained unruffled. Columba cried in a louder voice:

"O, monster of the loch, I bid you to appear before me."

Again, all present looked at the loch, but the waters remained unruffled. Columba cried in his loudest voice:

"O, monster of the loch, I bid you to appear before me!"

There was a silence. No one spoke or moved.

Then the surface of Loch Ness stirred. The waters surged apart and the monster reared up.

First its head.

Then its neck.

Then its body.

Then its tail.

When the people saw how huge it was, they fell to their knees trembling.

"Save us from the monster!" they begged Columba. "Save us from the monster!"

Columba pointed his staff at the monster and said:

I bid you be at peace with the air above you
I bid you be at peace with the earth below you
I bid you be at peace forever in the waters of the Deep.

The monster fixed its eyes on McKenzie. McKenzie nodded. Whereupon the monster bent its head and slid quietly under the water.

Columba declared that, although from time to time people might catch a glimpse of the monster, it would never seek to destroy them. Now and forever the monster of Loch Ness would be content to remain in the deepest waters of the loch.

The people thanked Columba for saving them from the monster. But after they had drifted off to their homes, Columba smiled and said to McKenzie, "I believe that, in this case, it is the monster who was saved from the people."

smoke curled from the hut

singing and splashing among the waves

when the moon rises but the sun hardly sets

came ashore and danced

soft breezes caused the waves to come lap, lap, lapping on the shore

Gillon and the Selkie

From the traditions of the Orkney Islands, selkie songs and stories tell of seals who can take off their skin and become human. Selkie tales are mostly about adults; it is good to have one that is about children.

Selkies are mysterious beings and so I thought I'd put a mystery inside this story for you...

Gillon lived with his mummy and daddy

on the sandy shores of the Orkney Islands.

His daddy was a fisherman, and Gillon was happy to help him bait the fishing lines and mend the nets. His mummy cooked the meals, cleaned the cottage and did the washing, and Gillon was happy to help her do this too.

24

He never went to bed hungry as there was always plenty of fish to eat: herring rolled in oatmeal or cod in parsley sauce; hake and haddock, mullet and mackerel, and teeny-tiny toasted sprats. They ate boiled fish and baked fish, frittered fish and cakes of fish, steamed fish and smoked fish, pan-fried and poached fish. And when they grew tired of eating fish, they would trade some of their catch for flour and eggs, and butter and sugar; then Gillon's mummy would make clootie dumplings and scones, and all manner of good things to eat.

Gillon loved living by the sea. In winter, fierce gales came roaring down from the cold north to send breakers crashing over the rocks. In summer, soft breezes caused the waves to come lap, lap, lapping on the shore. No matter what the weather did, Gillon liked to watch the water and listen to the sounds it made. He was a contented boy.

There was but one thing missing in Gillon's life. He had nobody to play with.

Still, there were lots of games he could play on his own. He jumped over the waves as they came rolling up the sand. He spread his arms, and ran around flapping his wings and making cries like the seabirds. His daddy carved him a wooden whistle and taught him how to coax a tune from it. When his mummy pegged the bedsheets on the drying line he'd chase in and out and under them, pretending they were ghosts and bogles trying to catch him. But his favourite place to be was in the treasure cave he'd made under the upturned hulk of a wrecked rowing boat. He'd sit on the old rug and blankets his mummy had allowed him to take from the cottage, and open the box his daddy had given him. Inside was a stump of driftwood shaped like a dragon, two picture books, three marbles, some odds and ends he'd found on the shore when the tide went out, and lots and lots of seashells. He'd never actually found any *real* treasure, like gold coins or precious jewels, but looking at the things in his box cheered him up when he was feeling lonely.

Sometimes Gillon wished so hard to have a friend he almost thought there was someone on the beach with him. He'd hear a chuckle when he filled the jug from the water barrel at the side of the cottage. There would be a sharp tug on the sheet as he helped his mummy peg it on the line. A shape would appear in the smoke that curled from the hut where they cured their fish.

When he told his mummy and daddy about this they smiled.

"It is the seagulls you are hearing," said his daddy. "They often make a noise that sounds as if they are laughing."

"It is the wind tugging on the sheet," said his mummy. "It blows constantly on our islands."

"And there are many different shapes to be seen in smoke," they both said. And they hugged Gillon, for they loved him very much.

Gillon knew that what his parents said made sense, but as he sat in his treasure cave he imagined someone whispering his name:

"*Gillon... Gillon... Gillon...*"

Midsummer Day is the longest day of the year – the time of the summer solstice – when the moon rises but the sun hardly sets, and sand and sea glitter gold and silver in the magical light. While eating his evening meal, Gillon looked from the cottage window and saw a group of seals swimming ashore. As he watched, they stood up on the sand, their grey sealskins fell from their bodies and they took the form of human people.

Gillon rushed to the door, for he wanted so much to go and play with the strange creatures who were now singing and splashing among the waves.

"Nay, nay," Gillon's daddy pushed the bolt across the door. "Best leave them in peace to do as their spirit bids them."

"You'd only frighten them away," Gillon's mummy told him.

Just then the wind grew stronger and the sea became choppy. The selkie people ran to put on their sealskins and dive into the water.

"Where are they going?" asked Gillon.

"To quieter waters on the other side of the island," said his daddy.

"Will we never see them again?" Gillon's voice was full of sadness.

"We might catch another glimpse," his mummy comforted him, "in the middle of winter on the shortest day of the year: the winter solstice."

29

The next morning Gillon rose early. It was always interesting to be on the beach after a storm. He picked up a chunk of green glass and squinted through it. He found a ball that still had some bounce left. He was rooting about among a tangle of seaweed when he heard a noise.

It was the sound of someone sobbing.

Gillon looked around. The sobbing was coming from his treasure cave in the upturned rowing boat. Gillon knelt down to peer inside. From the darkness, two wide dark eyes stared at him.

"Who are you?"

"I am a selkie," a girl's voice whispered.

"Why are you hiding in here?"

"I lost my sealskin. Without it I cannot go back into the water and swim away. Can you see it anywhere?"

Gillon looked along the beach. "No," he said. "And I have been searching the beach for treasure all morning."

"Treasure?" asked the selkie girl. "What kind of treasure?"

"Oh, this and that," said Gillon. "Why don't you come out and take a look for yourself. Together we might find your sealskin."

"I need some clothes to wear."

Gillon ran to the washing line and unpegged one of his shirts and a plaidie shawl that had been hung there to dry. The selkie girl put on the shirt and wrapped the plaidie shawl round her waist like a skirt. They searched the beach all day but they could not find the sealskin. Nor was there any trace of it in the days that followed. At night Gillon asked if he might have some food for his friend who'd come to live in his treasure cave.

His mummy smiled and said, "Of course you may."

His daddy patted his head and said, "Don't forget something to drink."

As the days and then the weeks passed, Gillon decided that he didn't really want to find the sealskin. He was enjoying himself too much. He taught the selkie girl to skim stones and she taught him to surf the waves. She showed him how to make a necklace from shells and he showed her how to make puzzles from knotted string. They had fun all day long, but if the selkie girl saw or heard anyone else on the beach she ran and hid beneath the boat.

They played together for the rest of the summer and into the autumn, until one evening Gillon's daddy came home with a piece of news:

"A schoolhouse has opened in the village. Children must go there and learn how to read and write, and count numbers up to one hundred and more."

"I do not want to go to school," said Gillon.

"But you will make friends at school," said his mummy.

"I have a friend already," said Gillon.

Gillon's daddy looked at Gillon's mummy and asked her, "Have you ever seen this friend that he speaks of?"

Gillon's mummy shook her head and said, "The sooner our son is in school the better."

Gillon went to school and he began to learn to read and write, and count numbers up to one hundred and more. But although he ran around the yard with his schoolmates during the day, when school was over he ran home as fast as he could to play with his selkie friend.

They played together for the rest of the autumn and into the winter, until one evening Gillon's daddy came home with another piece of news:

"You see that old cottage at the top of the cliff? A new family has moved in. There's a girl there of Gillon's age, and tomorrow she will be going along to the school."

That night the sun began to set early.

"It's the winter solstice," said Gillon's mummy, "the shortest day of the year."

"Will the selkies return tonight?" Gillon asked, while he collected food and drink to take to his treasure cave as he did every night.

"They might," said Gillon's daddy. "It's a night for strange happenings. See what I found among the fish I caught today." He held up what looked like a sheet of shimmering grey silk.

"What is it?" said Gillon's mummy.

"I truly do not know."

But Gillon knew exactly what it was. And he also knew what he must do with it. "May I have it?" he asked.

His daddy gave it to him and Gillon carried it, and the meal he'd prepared for the selkie girl, out into the gathering gloom.

"Don't delay too long," his mummy called after him. "You must come into the cottage before the selkies arrive on the beach."

The selkie girl gave a little sob as Gillon handed her the sealskin his father had caught with his fish. She held it to her cheek and stroked it. Then she looked at Gillon and whispered, "Thank you."

Gillon turned away before she would see the tears in his own eyes.

His parents watched with him as the seals came ashore and danced in their human forms by the seashore. But only Gillon saw the selkie girl creep from the upturned boat, skip lightly to the water's edge, don her sealskin and swim away. In the morning when Gillon's mummy opened their front door she exclaimed, "Oh, look Gillon! Look at what's lying on top of the old boat! It's that shirt of yours and my plaidie shawl that went missing from the washing line months ago. The wind must have blown them away and blown them back again."

Gillon scanned the sea as he walked to school that morning, but there was neither seal nor selkie in the wide waters.

33

There was a new girl in school. She was the one whose family had moved into the cottage on the cliff near where Gillon lived. The teacher placed her at the desk beside Gillon's and asked for her name.

"My name is Selah," said the girl in a soft voice.

"Why, that's a beautiful name," said their teacher. "Do you know what it means?"

"Yes, I do," said Selah. She turned and looked at Gillon. "It means: 'Let those with eyes, see, and those with ears, hear.'"

After school, Gillon walked home with the new girl. They parted at the top of the path that led down to the beach.

34

Gillon's mummy was standing outside their cottage. "Who is that?" she asked him.

"It's the girl from the family who have moved into the cottage on the cliff," said Gillon.

"Why don't you ask her to come down and play with you?"

Gillon raised his hand and waved. "Selah!" he called. "Would you like to come and play on the beach?"

The girl waved back and began to run towards him.

While Gillon waited for his new friend to join him he murmured her name again, *Selah*… And, as he did, he realised that 'Selah' sounds quite like 'Selkie'.

thick grass and heather of the Scottish hills

sliced long pillars from the black basalt stone cliffs

obliterated the mountain summit

Fiddle-dee-dee and fiddle-dee-dum

The Story of the Giant's Causeway

I have visited the Isle of Staffa in the Western Isles of Scotland, and the Giant's Causeway in Northern Ireland. When you look at the enormous paving stones stretching into the water at either end, it is very easy to believe that the path was made by giants who roared at each other across the sea!

This is a tale told long ago, when giants, both cruel and kindly, roamed the Earth.

In the Western Isles of Scotland there lived a giant called 'Benandonner'. In Ireland there lived a giant called 'Finn MacCool'. The Scottish giant was named Benandonner on account of his red hair. But why the Irish giant was named Finn MacCool I do not know, for I am a Scot. If you want to find out the answer to that question, you will have to ask an Irish person.

Benandonner and Finn were sometimes kind and sometimes cruel, but mostly they were just crabbit and bad tempered and often quarrelled with each other. As the whole width of the sea separated them they had to be content with yelling insults in loud voices.

"You're a tumshie!" Benandonner taunted Finn one day.

"And you, you are a bigger tumshie!" Finn replied.

"You are an even bigger tumshie!" Benandonner screamed, blowing thatches off cottages near where he lived, in a cave on the island of Staffa.

"You are the biggest tumshie there is!" Finn screeched, causing his cattle to hurtle through hundreds of hedges and land in Lough Neagh.

Losing his temper completely, Finn picked up a rock and chucked it over the water. It bounced off Benandonner's head.

Benandonner shook his fist at Finn and he bawled, "If I could swim, I would come and beat your hairy hide!"

"Come on then, why don't you?" Finn shouted. "To make it easy for you I'll build a bridge between our two countries, so I will."

"Go ahead then," said Benandonner. "If you dare."

Finn waited until nightfall when Benandonner would be asleep. Under a bright moon he set to work. He sliced long pillars from the black basalt stone cliffs next to his house. Then he chopped at the sides so they would have straight edges. He shaped them with six sides or more, to fit together like paving stones. And he made sure they were tall. He wanted them tall enough so that he could slam them deep down into the seabed, yet have their top ends sticking up above the surface of the water. Thus he was able to make a causeway that started at the northern tip of Ireland and stretched across the sea to where Benandonner lived in Scotland.

Finn had the path go right to Benandonner's front door inside his cave on Staffa.

After he'd finished he bounded home, calling back as he went, "Hey Benandonner! Now you have no namby-pamby excuse not to come over here and fight with me!"

When Benandonner saw what Finn MacCool had done, he clapped his hands in glee. So hard did he clap his hands that the blast of air obliterated the mountain summit of Dun Caan on Raasay, which is still flat to this very day.

Then Benandonner sang out:

Fiddle-dee-dee and fiddle-dee-dum,
Watch out Finn, here I come!

In Ireland, Finn spoke to his wife, Oonagh. "Look!" he said proudly. "I've made an easy path, which I can use to run to Scotland and take some of their cattle. I could snatch six sheep, three under each arm, and be home in time for dinner."

"But," said Oonagh, "I've heard tell that the Scottish giant is a giant among giants."

"That's just blarney," said her husband. "Everyone knows that the Scots are wee folk. I'll step on Benandonner and squish him flat."

"But," said Oonagh, "I've heard tell that the Scottish giant wears a kilt that is the size of all Ireland."

"Nay, woman," said Finn. "Stoke up the fire." He uprooted two large chestnut trees. "Here's some kindling to get the flames started. Boil the pot! Hee hee!" he laughed. "For our supper tonight we'll have Scots porridge made from a real Scot."

"But," said Oonagh, "I've heard tell that the Scottish giant can sit on Ben Nevis and paddle his feet in Loch Lomond."

"Nonsense," Finn scoffed, and taking great strides, he began to walk along the causeway.

It was nearly gloaming when Finn set out, with the sun sinking in the west. As he approached Scotland he saw an orange gleam in the sky.

"Ah!" he said, "It's a glorious sunset we are having this evening."

But it wasn't the sun setting. It was the top of Benandonner's head peeking up over the horizon, his carroty-red hair glowing.

"Ah!" said Finn, "There's the shine of water. It must be a Scottish river I see, sparkling in the light."

But it wasn't a river sparkling in the light. It was the eyes of Benandonner glistening with rage as he clenched his fists in anger.

"Ah!" said Finn, "There is the thick grass and heather of the Scottish hills."

But it was neither thick grass, nor was it heather. It was the two huge hairy legs of Benandonner showing beneath his kilt as he marched closer and closer to Finn MacCool.

The next minute Finn heard Benandonner bellowing:

Fiddle-dee-dee and fiddle-dee-dum.
Watch out Finn, here I come!

44

Finn looked up.
And up.
And up.
In all his life he had never seen such a gigantic giant. With a skip and a hop and a *very* long leap, Finn scarpered as fast as he could back to Ireland.

"What's wrong?" Oonagh cried when she saw him scuttling towards her.

"Help!" Finn shouted to his wife. "Help! Benandonner is coming."

"You wanted to fight him," said Oonagh. "So why are you running away?"

"He's a giant," stuttered Finn. "Benandonner is a *real* giant."

"So are you," said Oonagh and she hit him on the head with the ladle from the pot.

However, as soon as Finn's wife caught sight of Benandonner she said, "Even between us, we won't be able to beat him. What can we do?"

"Nothing." Finn sat down on a stool and began to wail.

Oonagh hit him on the head again with the ladle. Then, she took a sheet off their bed and quickly wrapped her husband up in it, round and round, until only the two eyes of his face were peeping out. Swaddled like a baby, she stuck him in the branches of a nearby oak tree.

When Benandonner pounded up to her house, Oonagh was bending over her swaddled husband. She was ladling soup into his mouth and crooning:

Hush my baby, do not fret thee,
Yer dadda won't let the Scottish giant get thee.

"Baby? Baby!" Benandonner looked at the enormous bundle nestling in the branches of the oak tree. "If that's your baby what size must his daddy be?"

"Finn MacCool's height is halfway to the moon," Oonagh answered him. "His girth would measure twice around the Mourne mountains."

"And this is his child?" Benandonner asked, his voice quavering.

"Oh yes," said Oonagh. "This one is just a wee bit laddie."

"Where is his father?" Benandonner glanced around in fear.

"His father, my husband, Finn MacCool, is on the road to Dublin to fetch his own two big brothers, for we are going to have a party."

"I won't keep you then," said Benandonner. "You'll want to prepare for your guests arriving."

"Stay on now," said Oonagh. "You can join us for singing and dancing."

"N-N-No. Thanks all the same," Benandonner stammered. "I must get home." And he hurried back to Scotland.

The following morning Benandonner thought more about the story Oonagh had told him, and he said to himself: "I'll just take another walk across there and see what's what."

But when he came out of his cave on Staffa, the causeway had vanished.

During the night Finn MacCool had pulled up his paving stones and cast them down into the depths of the sea. The waves washed over to sweep the rest away.

Today all that's left of the Giant's Causeway is its beginning and its end. The beginning is on the coast of County Antrim in Northern Ireland, where you can sit in Finn MacCool's giant wishing-chair. The end is on Staffa, a small island off the west coast of Scotland. Here you can visit the cave where Benandonner lived – which is now known as 'Fingal's Cave'.

swam fish of many colours

echoed with their ringing-singing sound

bind your promise with a kiss

gloaming light of half-dusk

the magic of making music

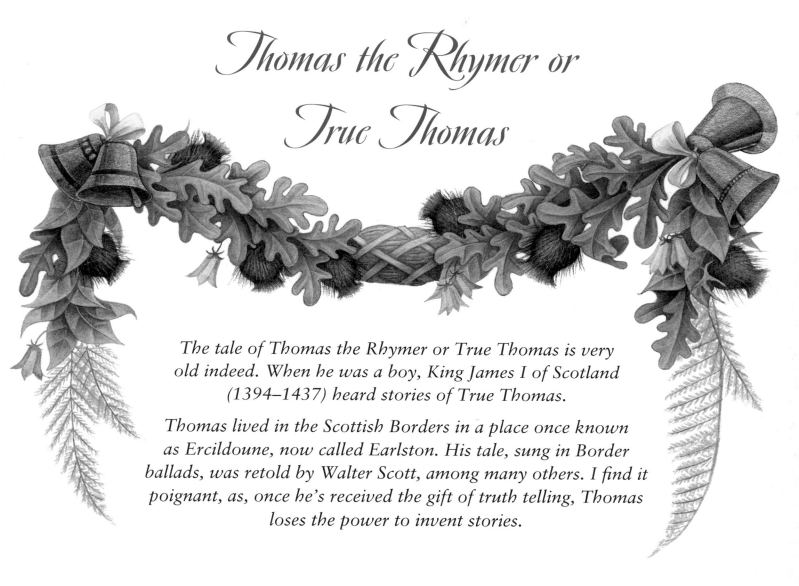

Thomas the Rhymer or True Thomas

The tale of Thomas the Rhymer or True Thomas is very old indeed. When he was a boy, King James I of Scotland (1394–1437) heard stories of True Thomas.

Thomas lived in the Scottish Borders in a place once known as Ercildoune, now called Earlston. His tale, sung in Border ballads, was retold by Walter Scott, among many others. I find it poignant, as, once he's received the gift of truth telling, Thomas loses the power to invent stories.

Nigh on seven hundred years ago,

in the Borderlands of Scotland, in the village of Ercildoune, lived a young man named Thomas.

Thomas was a minstrel. He wrote poems and set them to music. At feasts and fairs he would play upon his small harp to entertain folk. His verse made hearts soar, while his music shimmered through the air like a rainbow arching across the Earth. His songs were so melodic that he was known, both near and far, as 'Thomas the Rhymer'.

One warm summer morning, Thomas left his room in Learmont Tower and went a-wandering by the Huntly Burn. His father was holding a Midsummer Feast on the morrow and Thomas had promised to have a special ballad ready to celebrate the occasion, but the rhymes he required would not come into his mind. The sun blazed yellow in the sky above him and in every dale and dell of the Border countryside, trees and flowers bloomed: red, blue, green and gold. Thomas found a shady spot under the Eildon Tree and, taking his harp in his hand, he strummed upon the strings. As the day wore on, his head began to ache, for the words still eluded him. His eyelids drooped and he lay down on the grassy bank and fell asleep.

In the gloaming light of half-dusk, Thomas awoke with a start. It was late but not fully dark, for it was Midsummer's Eve: the time of the summer solstice, when the veil between the world of mortals and the world of the Other People is drawn aside.

Thomas sat up, wondering what had caused him to waken. He heard a ringing-singing sound and thought it to be the tinkling noise of water dashing over stones in the nearby Huntly Burn. Moonlight shone around the Eildon Tree and Thomas saw, riding towards him, a lady on a snow-white horse with a silver crown resting upon her head. She was robed in a flowing dress and cloak of emerald green. On her feet were velvet slippers with tiny bells sewn on the toes. Bells hung from the horse trappings and were plaited into its tail and mane. As she moved through the wood, the green glade echoed with their ringing-singing sound.

"Thomas!" The lady called his name in a sweet low voice.

"Who are you," replied Thomas, "that you so readily speak my name, yet I know not yours?"

"I am the Queen of Faeryland," the lady replied. She beckoned to him. "You must catch my stirrup and come with me."

Thomas thought the lady was the most beautiful creature he had ever seen and he had no hesitation in doing as she told him. He leaped to his feet. Slinging his harp over his shoulder he grasped the stirrup of her horse. The Queen of Faeryland bent her head and smiled at Thomas, and they went on their way.

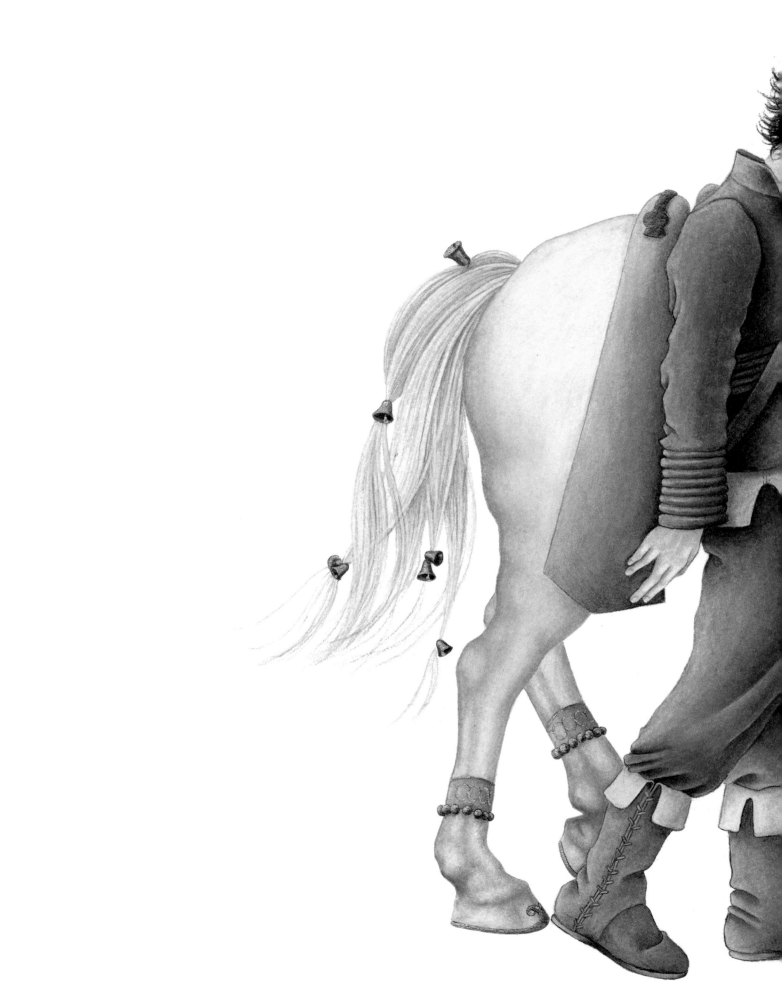

No word was spoken between Thomas and the Faery Queen as they journeyed together.

They travelled over a great river and in the water swam fish of many colours that Thomas had never seen before. They travelled through a thick forest and among the trees roamed wild beasts of a kind that Thomas had never seen before. They travelled past a city and in the streets walked people of a size and stature that Thomas had never seen before. His head was so filled with wonderment at the sights he saw that his senses reeled and speech stuck in his throat.

Then they came to a place where the road branched in three directions. The Queen of Faeryland drew rein on her horse and the ringing-singing sound of the bells stopped.

Thomas looked at the first path. It was a rough track overgrown with thorn bushes.

"What path is that?" he asked.

"The Path of Righteousness," replied the Faery Queen.

The second path was paved with smooth and shining cobblestones.

"What path is that?" Thomas asked.

"The Path of Wickedness," replied the Faery Queen.

The third path was a bonnie road that wound like a ribbon towards the Eildon Hills.

"What path is that?" Thomas asked.

The Faery Queen laughed softly and, urging on her horse, she rode along the third path.

"Where are you taking me?" asked Thomas, thrilled and frightened in equal measure.

The Queen of Faeryland laughed again. "Through the hollow hill to the Land of Everlasting Time."

Soon they arrived at the bottom of a cliff and the rock before them was flat and smooth with no crack or fissure upon it.

The Queen of Faeryland drew rein on her horse and the ringing-singing sound of the bells stopped.

"I will give you a warning, Thomas the Rhymer, and you must pay heed to what I say."

Thomas looked into the eyes of the Faery Queen and listened to what she told him in her sweet low voice.

"If you wish to return to your own country and your kin, then you must neither speak nor sup unless we are alone together."

Thomas was afraid, for he dearly loved his homeland of Scotland and his relatives and friends, and he feared to be parted forever from his country and his kin. But he desperately wanted to go through the hollow hill and see the Land of Everlasting Time. So he nodded in agreement.

"Then you may enter the realm of Faery, but first you must bind your promise with a kiss."

"This I will do willingly," said Thomas, "if you will make me a promise that you will take me back to my home in Ercildoune after I have counted the passage of seven days."

The Faery Queen nodded in agreement.

Thomas kissed the Queen of Faeryland to bind his promise to her that he would neither speak nor sup unless they were alone together.

The Queen of Faeryland kissed Thomas the Rhymer to bind her promise to him that she would return him to his home in Ercildoune after he had counted the passage of seven days.

Then the Queen of Faeryland raised her hand and pointed at the flat smooth surface of the rock with no crack or fissure upon it. The cliff face shuddered, a hidden door swung open, and the Faery Queen and Thomas entered in.

With a ringing-singing sound they trotted through Faeryland. The scent of honey filled the air and flowers were strewn in their path wherever they went. The Faery Queen led Thomas to her palace of gold and there he rested.

Every day was spent in composing verse with the Faery Queen and every night was spent in making music. It was easy for Thomas to remember to neither speak nor sup unless he and the Faery Queen were alone together. But it was not easy for Thomas to remember about the passage of time.

Such was the entertainment and so full was his happiness that Thomas almost forgot to count the days. To make sure he didn't overstay, every morning he strummed upon his harp and every evening he plucked out one of the strings. On the morning after he had plucked out the seventh string, no tune came from his harp when he tried to play it. Three times Thomas tried and three times the harp remained silent. Then Thomas understood that it was time for him to go home to Ercildoune. He spoke to the Queen of Faeryland.

"As I have kept my promise to you to neither speak nor sup unless you and I were alone together, it is time for you to keep your promise to take me back to my home in Ercildoune."

There were tears in the eyes of the Faery Queen as she replied, "A promise made and bound with a kiss must be kept. I said I would return you to your home in Ercildoune and that I will do."

No word was spoken between Thomas and the Faery Queen as they journeyed together.

Mounted on the snow-white horse, with a ringing-singing sound they left the golden palace and went through the hollow hill and out of the hidden door in the face of the cliff. Leaving the Realm of Faery and the Land of Everlasting Time, they trotted away from the Eildon Hills until they came to the place where the road branched in three directions. The Queen of Faeryland drew rein on her horse and the ringing-singing sound of the bells stopped.

Thomas looked at the first path, which was the rough track overgrown with thorn bushes.

"I do not choose the Path of Righteousness," he said.

Thomas looked at the second path, which was paved with smooth and shining cobblestones.

"I do not choose the Path of Wickedness," he said.

Thomas looked at the third path, which was a bonnie road that wound like a ribbon away from the Eildon Hills.

Before he could say anything more, the Faery Queen laughed softly and, urging on her horse, she rode along the third path in the direction of Ercildoune.

They travelled past the city where in the streets walked people of a size and stature that Thomas had seen before. They travelled through the thick forest where among the trees roamed wild beasts of a kind that Thomas had seen before. They travelled over the great river where in the water swam fish of many colours that Thomas had seen before. His head was so filled with wonderment at the sights he saw that his senses reeled and speech stuck in his throat.

In the gloaming light of half-dusk they reached the Huntly Burn and the grassy bank below the Eildon Tree. The Queen of Faeryland drew rein on her horse and the ringing-singing sound of the bells stopped.

"Ah," Thomas thought aloud. "I must find my father and apologise seven times for being seven days late for his Midsummer Feast."

The Queen of Faeryland bent her head and smiled at Thomas. "More than seven times seven will you have to apologise to your father."

"It will break my heart to leave you," Thomas told her, for he had fallen in love with the Faery Queen.

"As it will mine, for the same reason," replied the Faery Queen.

"Will I never see you again?" Thomas wept.

"We might yet be together," said the Faery Queen. "When the time comes for you to return to me, I will send you a sign."

"You must bind your promise with a kiss," said Thomas.

62

"That I will do," said the Faery Queen. "And in exchange for all the songs and music you have shared with me I will give a gift to you."

And so the Queen of Faeryland kissed Thomas and said:

The kiss I give to say goodbye
Ensures your tongue will never lie.

Thomas ran home. Bursting into the great hall of Learmont Tower he flung himself at his father's feet, saying, "Dearest Father, I am sorry that I am seven days late for your Midsummer Feast."

His father staggered back in amazement. "Dearest son," he said, "it is not seven days but seven years since you went missing from under the Eildon Tree." Then Thomas understood why the Faery Queen had said, "More than seven times seven will you have to apologise to your father."

Thomas's father was overjoyed to see him and bade him come to the table where he was dining with one of their neighbours. Thomas played his harp and tried to make up a verse to entertain them. The friend seemed pleased enough with his efforts, but to Thomas the song sounded empty of meaning and magic.

"I regret my wife was not fit to travel to hear your wonderful music," his father's friend told him.

Thomas looked up. As the words came from the man's mouth, Thomas could see the inside of his house. A woman sat beside a cradle that held a newborn babe.

"She would not want to leave your baby child," said Thomas.

The man gave Thomas a strange look. "How is it that you have news of the birth of my baby son when you have been gone from these parts for seven years?"

"I do not know," said Thomas. "Does your son sleep in a cradle of oak wood?"

"He does," replied the man. "But lots of cradles are made of stout oak wood."

"Does it have a canopy with your family crest embroidered on it?"

"It does," said the man. "It is my wife who did the needlework for she is skilled in this craft."

"Does your wife have the most lovely hair, black like a raven's wing?"

The man's face flushed in anger. "You are too familiar with your words about my wife!"

"It is what I can see," said Thomas.

Thomas's father cried out, "Dearest son, why do you speak this way? You are in danger of insulting our honoured guest."

But Thomas could not stop, for the Faery Queen had given him the gift of truth telling.

The kiss I give to say goodbye
Ensures your tongue will never lie.

"I see your wife in her bedchamber," said Thomas. The man stood up and reached for his sword.

"I see your son and your wife in the bedchamber," Thomas went on. "I see the scaffolding outside the window left by the builder repairing the roof. I see a small fire burning in the brazier. I see it tip over in the wind, and the wood of the scaffolding set alight."

"Fetch my horse!" the man shouted and he raced from Learmont Tower and rode off at full speed.

Upon arriving at his house an hour later the man rescued his wife and child just as the flames flickered against his bedroom window.

As news of the incident spread, people realised that Thomas had foretold the fire before it had actually begun.

From that day forth, instead of creating his own stories and songs Thomas spoke only of what he saw in his mind's eye. He wrote down these visions. Many of them came true and some have yet to happen.

Thomas's fame spread throughout Scotland and into the countries beyond. Nobles and knights, merchants and millers, and ordinary working folk visited him in Learmont Tower to seek his advice. In addition to being named 'Thomas the Rhymer' he also became known as 'True Thomas'.

Time passed – not seven hours, not seven days, not seven years – but seventy years. Thomas grew weary of bearing the burden of prophecy. His spirit yearned to wander once again in the realms of his imagination. His heart longed to recapture the magic of making music. More and more often he would climb to the top of Learmont Tower, look beyond the Eildon Tree, and sigh: "I think the Queen of Faeryland has forgotten her promise to come and take me back to the Land of Everlasting Time."

One day, on the eve of the winter solstice, when the veil between the world of mortals and the world of the Other People is drawn aside, a hunter came running into the hall of Learmont Tower.

"There is a white hind standing near the Huntly Burn. I stretched my bow to shoot an arrow at it. Suddenly my arm froze and for a minute I could not move. When I recovered I knew I must tell True Thomas this news."

Thomas left his room in Learmont Tower and walked to the Huntly Burn. Underneath the Eildon Tree was a pure white hind. On her head rested a silver crown. Thomas went close to the magical creature. And the shape of Thomas became the shape of the tree covered in white frost, and then, slowly, became the shape of a pure white hart.

Hart and hind stood by each other. They looked one last time at Ercildoune and the Eildon Tree and then they bounded away together towards the Eildon Hills. Snow began to fall, and from afar came echoing the ringing-singing sound of bells.

Northwards she flew

she looked to the south and saw Ireland shimmering in the disstance

a lady dressed in green and seated on a milk-white horse

Crawling along the earth

it has not kindness in its spirit, nor mercy in its mind

The Whirlpool of the Corryvreckan

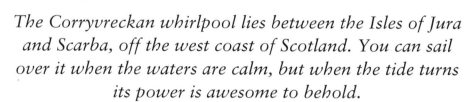

The Corryvreckan whirlpool lies between the Isles of Jura and Scarba, off the west coast of Scotland. You can sail over it when the waters are calm, but when the tide turns its power is awesome to behold.

Different tales are told as to how it came to be there. The word 'Corryvreckan' comes from the Gaelic coire *which means 'kettle'* or *'cauldron'* and breacan *which means 'shawl'* or *'plaid'*.

To tell my tale I've blended the story of the witch's shawl and the story of the loathsome Nuckelavee – a creature so horrible I can only whisper its name.

71

In the time before time, on the Isle of Skye

in a little croft at the foot of the Cuillin Mountains, there lived an old woman.

No one knew her real name, and she was so old that she herself had forgotten it. The people of Skye spoke of her in various ways, sometimes as 'the *cailleach*', which means 'the old woman', or '*bana-bhuise*', which means 'witch'. Perhaps she was a witch. She certainly owned a broomstick, and had been seen perched on it, flying over the Cuillins with her *breacan*, her long plaid shawl, streaming out behind her. She had a cauldron too – an enormous pot that hung above the fire she kept burning outside her door. Winter and summer, spring and autumn, she sat by this fire, crooning to herself whilst making porridge and potions. Her croft was known as the place of 'the *coire*', which means 'cauldron', and so, eventually, the old woman came to be called 'Corry'.

Corry was famed as a spae-wife throughout the Western Isles, for she had been in this world long enough to learn all that is known to mortals, and some of what is unknown. The islanders often went to her with their problems, both large and small. She was also wise in the ways of the Wee Folk. And it was said that, occasionally, they too knocked on the door of the croft under the Cuillins to seek her advice.

On the day of which I speak, more than one person made their way through the foothills to the croft of Corry.

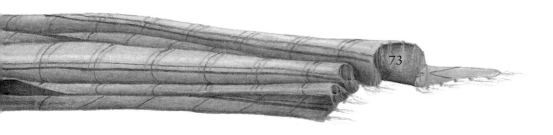

73

The first to arrive was a shepherd from Staffin. "During these last three nights, three of my sheep have been mauled on the hillside," he told Corry. "Please make a charm to keep away whatever mad dog is threatening my flock."

The second to arrive was a fisherman from Fada. "During these last two nights, two fishing boats have been wrecked while sitting safe in the harbour," he told Corry. "Please cast a spell to change the wild weather."

The third to arrive was a widow from Waternish. "During last night, one of my daughters became sick with a strange disease. Please mix a potion to restore her health."

Corry listened to what her visitors said and bade them return in two days.

That night, a lady dressed in green and seated on a milk-white horse rode by the cottage, singing in a mournful voice. Her song had no words but the tone was pleading, and Corry understood that the Wee Folk, too, needed her help.

As soon as it was light, Corry rose from her bed. Taking her *breacan* from the hook on the door she wrapped it seven times around her shoulders. Then she mounted her broomstick and flew into the air to survey the view in each direction.

She looked to the west and saw the watery waves of the great Atlantic Ocean, and all was as it should be there.

She looked to the east and saw the hills and heather of the mainland of Scotland, and all was as it should be there.

She looked to the south and saw Ireland shimmering in the distance, and all was as it should be there.

She looked to the north, towards the Faroe and the Orkney Islands. But there, all was not as it should be.

The sea was dark and oily and the shore was clogged with filth. From the north of the Isle of Skye, through Staffin, Fada and Waternish, a pestilence was spreading over the land. Corry flew home slowly.

She sat outside her door stirring her cauldron and pondering what this blight might be. When evening came she took a long, brightly lit piece of wood from the fire and, once again wrapping her *breacan* seven times around her shoulders, she mounted her broomstick and set off north. Hither and thither she flew until she spied a shape moving on a rough track below her. She dropped the blazing torch.

As the torch plunged down, its light shone over the ground revealing a horrible sight. Crawling along the earth was the most hideous creature, with splayed legs and long muscular arms. There was no skin on the surface of its body, only red-raw flesh. Within the flesh were veins of glaring yellow, and in them ran tar-black blood. The creature raised its huge head and a single eye glowed like a flaming beacon. Snatching the flaring torch, it threw it to the ground and trampled out its light.

The next morning the shepherd, the fisherman and the widow came to the croft under the Cuillins. But Corry had prepared nothing to give them.

"Neither charm, nor spell, nor potion will cure what ails our island," she told them. "For it is not a mad dog, nor wild weather, nor a strange disease that is the cause of your troubles. It is something much worse."

"What is it?" they asked.

Corry looked at them and, for the first time, the islanders saw fear in the eyes of the old woman. "A terrible creature has swum ashore from the northern waters to bring pestilence and death amongst us."

"Does this creature have a name?" they asked her.

"Yes," said Corry. "It is a Nuckelavee."

Upon hearing this the shepherd, the fisherman and the widow grew pale. Stories of the dreadful Nuckelavee were frequently told round the hearth. It was a vile creature – the cause of floods and famine, of disasters and droughts – whose sole purpose was to destroy everything in its path.

"It has the strength of twenty men and more," said the shepherd. "It will crush everything it meets."

"It is too dangerous for anyone to approach it," said the fisherman. "It will leave us lamenting in its wake."

"It has no kindness in its spirit, nor mercy in its mind," said the widow. "My child and others will surely die."

Corry nodded her head. "It is true that it is strong. It is true that it is dangerous. It is true that it has no kindness in its spirit, nor mercy in its mind." She hesitated and then said, "It is also true that the Nuckelavee can never be killed."

The shepherd, the fisherman and the widow fell to weeping and wailing. They cried out, "We are doomed!"

"Perhaps," said Corry. "Perhaps not. What cannot be killed can yet be curtailed. The Nuckelavee moves about in the dark, for it cannot bear the light. It drinks from the sea, for it cannot stand the touch of pure water. It cannot be caged, for it spins round and round without stopping if captured." She paused. "Listen carefully to what I am about to say and then do exactly as I ask you."

To the shepherd she said, "Bring me wool from the sheep that were mauled on the hillside."

To the fisherman she said, "Bring me twine from the boats that were wrecked in the harbour."

To the widow she said, "Bring me hair from the head of your daughter who is sick with a strange disease."

To all three of them she said, "Bring these things to me before nightfall."

As the shepherd and fisherman and the widow left the croft they heard Corry mutter these words:

Water clear as clear can be
Will defeat the Nuckelavee.

While they were gone, Corry was not idle.

She emptied her cauldron and scrubbed it clean. Then she fetched bucket after bucket of pure clear water from a mountain spring to fill it.

The moon was rising as the shepherd, the fisherman and the widow returned carrying the items they had collected. Corrie wove the wool from the mauled sheep, the twine from the wrecked boats and the hair from the head of the sick girl together with the moonbeams, to make a stout rope.

That night, a lady dressed in green and seated on a milk-white horse rode by the cottage, singing in a sweet voice. Her song had no words but Corry understood that the Wee Folk would lend her their strength to carry out the task she must perform on the morrow.

The sun's rays were about to touch the slopes of the Cuillins when Corry took her *breacan* from the hook on the door and looped it over one arm. Over her other arm she looped the stout rope. And over the end of her broomstick she looped the handle of her cauldron, which was full of pure water from the mountain spring.

Northwards she flew, until she got to the place where the creature was ravaging the land. In the half-dark she could see it scuttling along the ground and Corry knew she must act now, before the daylight came and it hid itself away. Swooping low, she tilted the cauldron so that the water might run out. But the Nuckelavee spotted her and lashed out with its long arms. Corry sped past, then turned her broomstick to renew her attack. This time she dived from above. Plummeting towards the creature she emptied out the contents of her cauldron. Like a long waterfall the pure water poured down, splashing on to the red-raw flesh of the Nuckelavee.

The Nuckelavee bellowed with rage. Then it opened its mouth and let out a loud roar, belching a foul stench and furnace heat. Corry did not flinch. As the fresh mountain water soaked into it, the creature started to shrink and shrivel.

Corry spread wide her *breacan* and flung it to the earth, covering the creature. Trapped inside the plaid, the Nuckelavee twisted this way and that way, trying to get free. Corry landed beside it. Gathering up the four ends of her *breacan*, she fastened them with her stout rope of wool, twine, hair and moonbeams. She pushed the bundle into her cauldron and, mounting her broomstick, she took off into the air in the direction of the Cuillins.

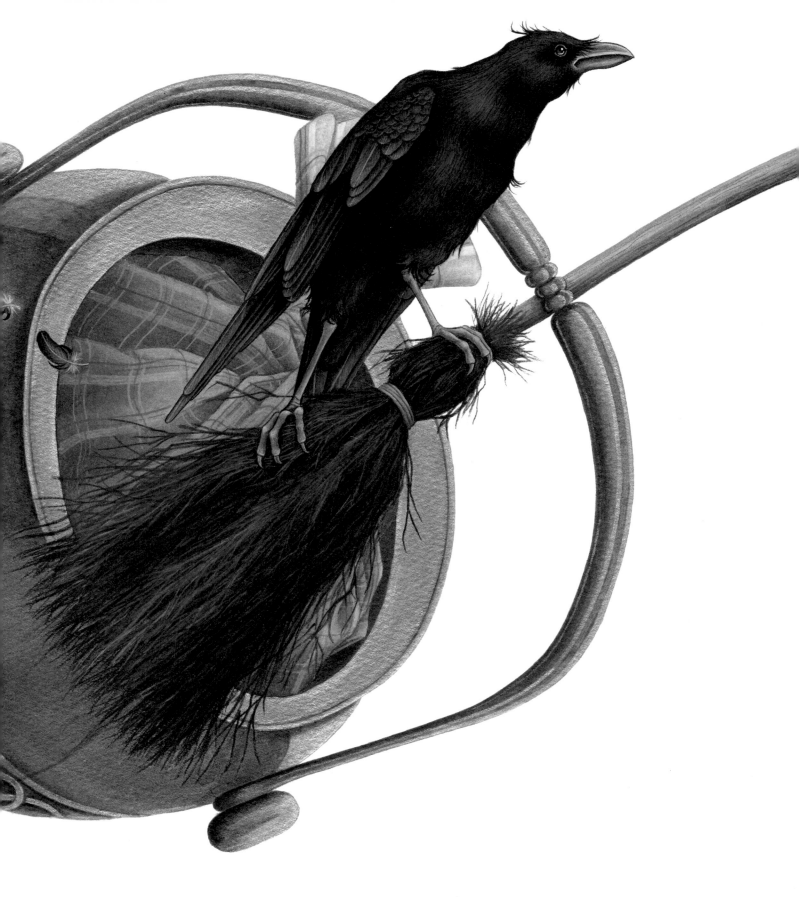

But even when shrunk and shrivelled, a Nuckelavee is powerful. Corry struggled to keep herself steady as the creature writhed about, bending the broomstick to breaking point. The weight of the cauldron with the Nuckelavee inside it began to drag her down. The broomstick shuddered. Corry clung on, fearing that the Nuckelavee would escape if the cauldron smashed upon the mountainside. A rocky precipice loomed ahead. She was going to crash!

But suddenly she heard the sound of voices singing. The song had no words but the air was full of magic and Corry understood that the Wee Folk had come to her aid and would lift her up.

Fast and furious, onwards and upwards, Corry flew, until she reached the top of the mountain known as Sgurr Alasdair. Dismounting quickly, Corry grasped the handle of the cauldron. There, on the highest peak on Skye, she whirled round and round – not three, but thirty-three times. Then Corry let go.

First the cauldron streaked through Skye. Then, travelling in a wide circle, it louped into Lewis and hurtled past Harris. South it went, down to North Uist, Benbecula, and South Uist. It bounced beyond Barra and careered across Coll and Colonsay.

Finally it jumped over Jura where, spinning round and round, it stotted into the sea just short of Scarba.

And in that stretch of water the cauldron is still spinning today, which is why the whirlpool in the strait between Jura and Scarba is known as *Coire Breacan*, or 'the Corryvreckan'.

blown onto the Bell Rock and torn asunder

whip the water up into mountainous waves

bodies are covered in silver scales

they dare not be in the light

With a tremendous judder the ship struck hard, and stuck fast.

sharp pebbles and slippery cobblestones

The Mermen of the Bell Rock

The Bell Rock is the topmost part of a long and dangerous reef that lies on a main shipping line in the North Sea, eleven miles east of Arbroath. The surface of the reef is uncovered only at low tide, while at high tide it is submerged just under the water, which means that sailors cannot see the terrible danger.

Robert Southey wrote a poem about how, long ago, a pirate stole the warning bell which the Abbot of Arbroath had placed upon the rock. Others say that the bell was torn down by mermen who wanted to wreck passing ships. Mermen, with scaly skins, and claws for hands…

In the gurly grey waters of the North Sea,

off the east coast of Scotland between the Firth of Forth and the Firth of Tay, lurks the deadly dangerous Bell Rock.

Of all the hazards facing sailors who travel on that busy shipping route, it is the very worst. This massive jagged rock can rip open the hull of the stoutest ship and within seconds send it to the bottom of the sea. The Bell Rock is doubly terrifying because as well as being massive and jagged, for most of the time its full length lies hidden just under the surface of the water and cannot be seen. In olden days many a ship foundered there – in a single year seventy vessels were wrecked – and many a family was left to mourn the loss of a loved one.

And it was in olden days, when the perilous spot was known as 'the Inchcape Reef', that the Abbot of Arbroath attempted to bring an end to these disasters. He ordered the bell to be taken from the bell tower of the abbey, carried to the port and placed in a boat.

86

Then, at low tide, while the reef was uncovered for a few hours, he himself sailed out there and, with strong ropes, fastened the bell to the biggest rock.

Those who watched the Abbot do this cheered and clapped their hands.

To begin with, his plan worked. When the wind was fierce the tolling of the bell carried above the roar of the sea surging over the reef. Fishermen and sailors, merchant ships and warships heeded the signal and avoided the area. They gave thanks for the Abbot of Arbroath Abbey, and the Inchcape Reef came to be known as 'the Bell Rock'.

But one morning the bell was gone – stolen by a pirate, some said. And, although the reef was still called the Bell Rock, no longer did pealing notes ring their warning; no longer did captains of ships hear the sound and stay away. Once again the treacherous rock claimed the lives of mariners who did not know the safest route, and also of those who thought they did – for in stormy weather, ships trying to bypass the danger were blown on to the Bell Rock and torn asunder.

Storms in that part of the North Sea are truly dreadful. Gale-force winds bring rain and hail lashing down from the sky and whip the water up into mountainous waves. Although eleven miles out to sea, the loud booming noise made by the heavy swell battering and crashing against the Bell Rock means the people in fishing villages, and even inland county towns, can hear it.

Nigh on two hundred years ago, there was a storm so terrible that the fisher folk at the harbour heard it, the farm folk heard it, and, in the wee cottage on the sands at Arbroath where she lived with her grandmother, Catriona heard it too.

"It was a wicked pirate indeed," said Catriona, "who stole the alarm bell from the Bell Rock."

"'Twas not a wicked pirate who stole it," said Catriona's grandmother. "It was the mermen who live in the waters around the Bell Rock. They cut the strong ropes and cast the bell into the sea."

"I hope no sailors are in a ship near the Bell Rock tonight," Catriona went on. "But if they are, then I hope that their captain is a canny and clever man."

"The best sea captain in the world will be unable to save his ship if it is seized by the Mermen of the Bell Rock," Catriona's grandmother told her. "The mermen have no mercy. With their lobster-like claws they hack huge holes in the hulls of passing ships so that the water rushes in and causes the vessels to sink."

"Is there no way that the sailors in the ships can chase off the mermen?" asked Catriona.

"It's hard to see the mermen. They hate the light and wait until it is gloomy before coming to the surface. Their bodies – half-man, half-fish – are covered with silver scales and their greenish-brown hair looks like seaweed trailing in the water."

"We should put an extra lamp in our window," Catriona said to her grandmother, "for a ship at sea might see the glow and steer a course towards the harbour."

But when the storm was finally over, there was no ship safe in the harbour, just wreckage washed up on the incoming tide. For that storm had been the most violent storm ever. Day and night it raged, with thunder rolling in the heavens above, and the seas boiling below. And during it, ploughing north through the waves from England came a ship of the line carrying three hundred sailors. Unknown to them and their captain, the Bell Rock lay directly in their path. To the lookout on the topmast peering through the gloom, nothing was visible. It was only when they were almost upon it that a flash of lightning revealed the glistening ragged rock right beneath them.

The lookout screamed a warning.

Too late! With a tremendous judder the ship struck hard, and stuck fast.

Alas! Although the sailors fought bravely to haul away from the Bell Rock, their ship smashed in pieces and went down with all hands. Three hundred men lost their lives and there was weeping and wailing at humble hearths and high homes throughout the land.

And throughout the land people complained and bemoaned the enormous number of deaths. Everyone asked the same question: What could be done about the Bell Rock? And everyone gave the same answer: Nothing. Nothing could be done about the Bell Rock.

Their talk reached the ears of the government who held meetings to discuss the problem. Eventually engineers were commissioned to investigate the possibility of building a lighthouse upon the Bell Rock.

"Build a lighthouse!" Catriona's grandmother exclaimed. "The Mermen of the Bell Rock won't allow that to happen. They are creatures of the dark, who detest light, for it shrivels their skin and burns the eyes from their heads. If a lighthouse was built there they would never be able to live in those waters."

"Then we must help with the lighthouse in any way we can," Catriona declared.

Skilful men were sent to assess the project of the Bell Rock Lighthouse. From outside their cottage door, where she and her grandmother sat mending nets for the fishermen, Catriona watched them.

These men recorded high tides and low tides. They sailed out to the Bell Rock and noted how it only appeared above the surface of the sea for a short time each day. They took readings of wind speed and watched the swirling currents. They looked and pointed and measured. Many came and many shook their heads and went away.

And then, a Mr Stevenson from the city of Glasgow arrived. He was an engineer who had built lighthouses in the Orkney Islands and the River Clyde.

He recorded high tides and low tides. He sailed out to the Bell Rock and noted how it only appeared above the surface of the sea for a short time each day. He took readings of wind speed and watched the swirling currents. He looked and pointed and measured. Then he, too, went away.

But he came back again.

And again.

And again.

This engineer was a courteous man. When he passed Catriona and her grandmother sitting on the sands he would raise his hat in greeting. Occasionally he stopped to talk about the weather forecast and always listened attentively to their opinion on local conditions.

He admired the complicated knots they tied to close up larger holes in the fishing nets, and drew these in his notebook. Then he showed them some other pages where he was working out the dangers of his project.

When Catriona's grandmother realised that this engineer was determined to build a lighthouse on the Bell Rock she said quietly to Catriona, "His plan is doomed. The mermen will not be defeated."

"Perhaps he hasn't heard of the mermen," said Catriona. "I could tell him."

"He might not believe you."

Catriona waited until the engineer was sitting alone on the beach reading his notebook. She approached and stood before him. "Please sir," she spoke up bravely. "You must add the Mermen of the Bell Rock to your list of dangers."

The engineer raised his head and smiled at her. "I've been warned of the howling hurricanes, and the swiftly changing tides. I've been told that this is the most treacherous submerged shipping hazard in the whole wide world. But no one has mentioned the Mermen of the Bell Rock. Who are these mermen?"

"They have the tail of a fish, but the chest, head and arms of a man. Instead of hands they have cruel claws like those of a lobster. They rip open the hulls of ships so that the water rushes in and then they drag the sailors out to drown them."

"Is there no way that the sailors in the ships can chase off the mermen?"

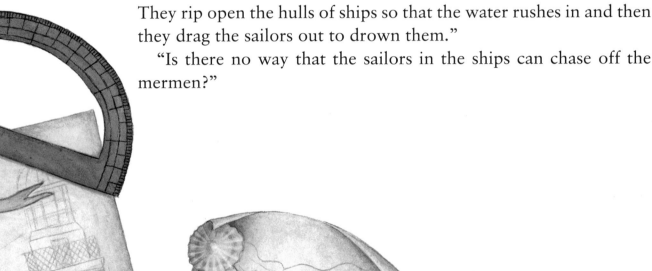

"Their bodies are covered in silver scales and their hair is greenish-brown and tangled, so when folks do catch a glimpse of them, they think it to be seaweed floating in the water. Mermen hide in the depths of the sea, for they dare not be in the light. No one can see them properly."

"This is the worst danger I have heard of," said the engineer. "Thank you for telling me about it."

"They like to wreck boats. Long ago, when the Abbot of Arbroath tied a warning bell on their rock, they cut the strong ropes and cast the bell into the sea."

"I will not put a bell there. Instead we will put a light. A brilliant light that will be seen for fifty miles in all directions."

"Mermen hate light," said Catriona. "It causes their skin to shrivel and their eyes to burn. They will screech in anger and try to tear it apart. Please make your lighthouse sturdy."

The engineer looked at her with a kindly face and said very seriously, "My lighthouse will be exceptionally sturdy. I will use the best of materials to build it." He wrote down everything Catriona had told him in his notebook, and then he said, "You remind me of my son, Thomas, who has a powerful imagination. He loves hearing and telling stories."

The engineer was true to his word.

He did use the best of materials to build the lighthouse: solid blocks of granite and metals forged in foundry fire. Because the Bell Rock was only uncovered for a few hours each day, the workmen had to be prepared to land there when they could, and get off again as soon as the water level rose. A large boat named the *Smeaton* was to be moored near the Bell Rock, and the engineer, the workmen and the equipment would stay on it when the tide was high. There would be three small boats, all of which were needed to transfer the men to the rock and back to the *Smeaton*. Also, to help illuminate the site, the engineer intended to set up a floating light.

"Ah!" Catriona's grandmother gripped the engineer by the hand when he told her this. "As soon as you do that the mermen will attack you."

"It is a risk worth the taking," he replied, "for we must prevent the sea from claiming any more victims."

"Please be careful," Catriona begged.

"I will. I will," the engineer promised them, and he strode off to the harbour to board the *Smeaton*.

As they watched the ship sail towards the Bell Rock, Catriona's grandmother turned to her. "We must make a fishing net," she said, "a special net, closely woven. I will go to the pilot at the harbour, who knows the Bell Rock better than anyone, and ask him for copper wire. We will tie this net with our strongest knots."

And so Catriona and her grandmother sat on the sands and made a special fishing net of copper wire, closely woven and tightly tied with special knots. It was finished on a September morning when dense dark cloud thickened the air and the mood of the sea was strange and sinister.

Catriona's grandmother gathered the net into a bundle and gave it to her. "You must run as fast as you can to the pilot at the harbour and ask him to take this net to the Bell Rock and give it to the engineer. Tell him that I sent you and he will understand that it must be done at once."

Ignoring sharp pebbles and slippery cobblestones, Catriona ran swiftly on her bare feet to the harbour and gave the net and her grandmother's message to the pilot.

The tide was on the turn as the pilot set out and, by the time he reached the Bell Rock, the water was lapping over its surface and rising rapidly higher.

The pilot expected that the men would have stopped for the day and be on their way back to the *Smeaton* in the three small boats. To his shock he saw the engineer and the thirty-six workmen clustered by the landing place. They were in the gravest peril, for only two boats were there to take them off the rock. There was not enough room for everyone to get on board. The pilot glanced seawards and saw that the *Smeaton* had slipped her moorings and, with the third small boat attached, was drifting away. Had he not arrived at that moment, some of the marooned men would have drowned.

"It was your action and your net that surely saved us," the engineer told Catriona and her grandmother. "The pilot threw the net and I caught it. We secured it to the rock, grabbed firm hold and clung on as the tide swamped us. Thus we were anchored as we waited to be ferried to the safety of the pilot boat." He gazed at Catriona's grandmother. "How did you know that I needed help that day?"

"That I cannot tell you for I do not know myself," she answered.

"But we knew that the mermen would disturb your work," said Catriona.

The engineer showed them the frayed rope that had caused the *Smeaton* to come loose from its moorings. "I would say that this rope chafed against the rough edge of the rock and thus snapped in two. What say you?"

"That rope was split and shredded by the mermen," said Catriona. "They sawed at it with their lobster claws so that your boats would be cast adrift and you might die upon the Bell Rock."

"My head would deny that tale," the engineer spoke slowly, "yet your story resonates within my heart." He paused. "And it is curious that the first lumps of granite we managed to place upon the rock were overturned during the night and flung into a crevice, and the forge we set up was bent and twisted."

"You could use our net to cover whatever goods you leave upon the rock," Catriona suggested. "It would be difficult for the mermen to slash it open."

"That is indeed what I will do," said the engineer and he thanked Catriona and her grandmother for their good advice.

From then on, the materials unloaded onto the Bell Rock remained unscathed.

The work continued and the body of the lighthouse grew tall into the sky. It took almost four years before the first lamp was lit atop the sturdy white tower. And the light could be seen for fifty miles in all directions – a blazing red-and-white revolving beacon to dazzle the eyes.

If anyone had listened, they would have heard the mermen shrieking in fury as they fled from the Bell Rock, never to appear in those waters again.

To this day, off the east coast of Scotland between the Firth of Forth and the Firth of Tay, the Bell Rock Lighthouse shines out its warning signal to keep shipping safe in the gurly grey waters of the North Sea.

Half a hundred years after the lighthouse was built, when Catriona was herself a grandmother, she still sat mending nets on the sands at Abroath. One summer there was a group of people on the beach.

"It's the Stevenson family," somebody told her. "They've brought the lighthouse builder's grandson here, for his lungs are weak and they hope that the sea air will do him good."

Catriona judged the boy to be around eight years old. "I met your grandfather when I was your age." She smiled at him and pointed to the Bell Rock Lighthouse. "By building that lighthouse your grandfather saved many lives."

"I know," the boy replied. "My father told me this. He reads to me from my grandfather's notebooks – not just about how he built the lighthouse, but also the stories he wrote down. I like stories. I like them very much."

"So do I," said Catriona. "My grandmother was good at telling stories."

"That's what I am going to be when I grow up," said the boy, "a storyteller."

"My name is Catriona," she told him.

"I like that name," said the boy. His bright eyes shone with interest and imagination.

"Will you tell me yours?" she asked.

In answer the boy took a stick and he wrote in the sand,

Robert Louis

Stevenson

The sky darkened as an enormous winged Beast with hooked talons, glittering eyes

He set his arrow alight and shot it straight and true

awful crunching noise

sound like rolling thunder, the Beast flapped its leathery wings

The Archer and the Island Beast

'The Archer and the Island Beast' is an old clan tale from the northeast of Scotland that is similar to the story of William Tell.

The Thane of Moray was
a cruel and greedy man.

He ruled his fiefdom of Elgin in the north of Scotland neither wisely nor well. The people on his lands lived in poverty, for he made them pay heavy taxes and did not look after them, though this was his duty.

In the Thane's fiefdom there was a small stretch of water known as Loch Loy. It was surrounded by thick forest, fertile fields and a pretty village.

Near the village there lived a boy. His home was a rough wooden shelter he had made for himself at the edge of the forest. He had no parents or grandparents, nor indeed any family whatsoever. As he had neither kith nor kin, he had no name, and was always referred to as 'the Boy'. The Boy could hunt better than anyone else in the area and was supremely skilled with arrow and bow. Using a single arrow he could bring down a running rabbit in a field, or the swiftest deer in the forest. Often, he gave what he caught to the children of the village.

Each autumn, when flocks of migrating birds came to the tiny island in the middle of Loch Loy, the Boy would help the villagers capture some of them. He'd dip an arrowhead in the bucket of pitch that stood beside the village fire, and lift a glowing peat and place it in a clay pot. Taking these with him, he'd hide in a rowing boat and let the current ferry him over to the island. When he got there, he'd set the arrow alight and fire it amongst the birds. Everyone waited with their nets spread, in the happy hope of trapping a tasty meal for Christmastide.

The villagers were grateful for any extra food the Boy could provide, for all those who lived under the rule of the Thane were growing poorer and hungrier.

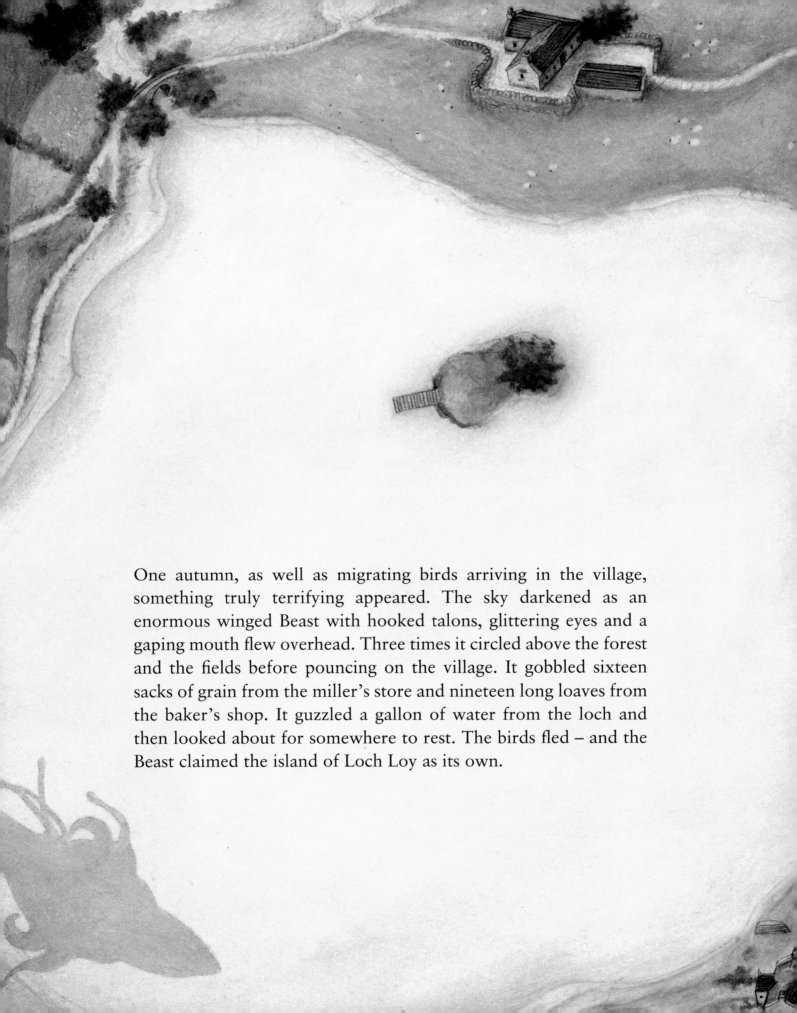

One autumn, as well as migrating birds arriving in the village, something truly terrifying appeared. The sky darkened as an enormous winged Beast with hooked talons, glittering eyes and a gaping mouth flew overhead. Three times it circled above the forest and the fields before pouncing on the village. It gobbled sixteen sacks of grain from the miller's store and nineteen long loaves from the baker's shop. It guzzled a gallon of water from the loch and then looked about for somewhere to rest. The birds fled – and the Beast claimed the island of Loch Loy as its own.

The Island Beast was lazy and not inclined to fly far, or indeed leave the island, to find food to eat. But it had no need to. The local villagers were so scared of the Island Beast that they made sure it was fed regularly. Every week they piled the Beast's dinner onto a small boat and sent it sailing over to the island. During the course of the next seven days the Beast would eat the food on the boat, and occasionally, if it was especially hungry, it ate the boat too.

When the people heard the awful crunching noise of the Beast's teeth munching through the boat, and saw the splinters and broken pieces of wood floating in the water, they tried to make sure that the Beast had even more food the following week. If they did not manage to do this then the Beast would roar in anger, stagger to its feet, and take off into the air. As the noise echoed round the loch, the village children ran, screaming, to hide indoors. With a sound like rolling thunder, the Beast flapped its leathery wings and swooped low over the rooftops to snatch a dog or a cat, and once even an old woman who was warming herself by the village fire.

112

113

The news of this reached the ears of the Thane of Moray in his castle. He decided he would have to rid his fiefdom of the Island Beast. This wasn't because the people in the area of Loch Loy were in danger or might starve to death – he didn't care about that. What worried him was that if the villagers finished all their supplies, they would not be able to pay their taxes to him.

And so the Thane of Moray called for his guards and he marched with them to Loch Loy. At first the people of Loch Loy were glad when their Thane arrived. They thought he had come to battle against the Island Beast. But the Thane made himself and his men comfortable in their houses and he ordered the villagers to go and slay the Beast. The people begged him to send his guards to kill the Beast, but the Thane refused, saying that he would not risk the lives of his well-trained men. However, he offered to lend the villagers swords and shields to help them fight the Island Beast. The villagers pointed out that they did not know how to use swords and shields as they were not soldiers. At this the Thane laughed, and said the sooner they learned the better. He told his guards to put a few of the villagers in a boat and set its course to the island. They did not come back. The Thane sent some more. They also did not return.

When the Thane heard of the Boy who was so accurate in his aim that he never missed his target, he sent for him and said, "I order you to go to the island in Loch Loy and kill the Island Beast."

The Boy looked at the Thane of Moray and said, "What if I refuse?"

"You will die where you stand!" the Thane shouted, furious that the Boy should question his order.

"I do not fear death," the Boy said quietly.

The Thane sneered at him. "I will burn down the village and the forest. I will drive off the cattle and destroy the crops in the fields. I will make slaves of these people and their children."

The Boy looked at the Thane of Moray and said, "Very well. I will obey your order."

The Thane was angry at the Boy's manner and he decided to punish him. "Let us see how marvellous a hunter you really are," he said. "You will be allowed to take only one arrow with you to the island."

The Boy selected an arrow from his quiver and examined it carefully. He laid it down near the bucket of pitch by the village fire. Then he chose another arrow, dipped it into the pitch bucket, and this one, along with a glowing peat in a clay pot, he took with him. He left the first arrow behind.

The villagers made ready the boat that ferried the supplies to the Island Beast.

Many of them, particularly the children, wept on seeing the Boy climb aboard. The boat was packed with three cows, two hogs and a duck. The Boy lay down and hid himself while the boat was cast loose to drift with the currents across the waters of Loch Loy.

When it bumped onto the island the Boy peeped over the rim of the boat. The huge head of the Beast was directly in front of him! He peered closer. The Beast was sleeping. If he was to kill the Island Beast using only one arrow, it had to be awake – and it might attack him. He had faced wild animals in the forest, but none like this. The Boy's heart began to beat hard in his chest. Then he thought of the village children becoming slaves of the ruthless Thane and he summoned his courage for what he must do.

First he chased the three cows off the boat. The cows wandered towards a field, mooing at the sight of the green grass.

The Island Beast opened one eye a tiny bit. "Ah," it grunted. "There is the main course of my meal."

Next the Boy pushed the two hogs off the boat. The hogs ran directly for a large rain puddle, snorting at the sight of the deep mud.

The Island Beast opened its other eye a tiny bit. "Ah," it growled. "There is the dessert course of my meal."

Last of all the Boy flapped his hands so that the duck flew off the boat and came to rest by the shoreline, quacking at the sight of clear water.

The Island Beast opened both eyes and its mouth too. "Ah," it bellowed. "This will be the starter course of my meal." It stretched its neck towards the water to eat the duck with a single gulp.

The Boy stood up. He set his arrow alight and shot it straight and true. The blazing arrow flew down the Beast's throat and pierced its heart right through. With a hideous howl the Island Beast's head crashed to the ground and the thud shook the whole island.

When the people of Loch Loy saw the Boy returning, they cheered loudly and, raising him onto their shoulders, they carried him to the village.

In the centre of the village the Thane waited with his arms folded. Everyone was rejoicing. But the Thane was not pleased. He could see that the villagers loved the Boy and that by slaying the Island Beast he would gain great fame and influence. This Boy could easily become their leader. Because he was brave and good, people would follow him. And eventually they might rebel against their Thane.

Then the Thane of Moray noticed the arrow the Boy had left behind near the bucket of pitch by the village fire. He pointed to it.

"Explain to me," he addressed the Boy, "why you laid an arrow there before you went to slay the Island Beast. What was the purpose of that arrow?"

The Boy picked up the arrow and he looked at the Thane of Moray and said, "If I had missed the Beast but had managed to escape, I would have used this arrow to kill you."

The Thane of Moray smiled. And his smile was more terrible than his anger.

"Seize him!" he cried.

The Boy slotted the arrow into his bow, took steady aim and said, "If any man moves towards me, you die. Go from here and leave my people alone."

The Thane realised that he would have no more power if he allowed himself to be bested by an upstart boy.

"My men will not move against you," he said. "They will move against your friends." And he made a sign with his hand to his guards, who immediately seized several of the children.

119

"You may kill me," said the Thane. "But if you do, these children, too, will die."

The Boy hesitated. He gripped his bow more tightly. Slowly he drew back the bowstring. The fathers yelled and the mothers shrieked, but the children remained still, for they knew the Boy. Had he not fed them secretly when they were hungry? Had he not made them bows and arrows so they too could learn to hunt? They trusted the Boy, and watched him calmly.

Quickly the Boy dipped the arrow point in the pitch bucket and lit it from the fire. Then he let it go, shooting the flaming arrow high into the air.

The Thane's men grabbed him and he was dragged off to the castle. The Thane announced that the people must assemble there in the morning where the Boy would be executed for rebellion against his overlord.

It happened that the King of Scotland and his army were approaching the lands of Moray. His messengers had reported the presence of the Island Beast, and he was making his way north with his soldiers to see whether he could help the people.

The King spotted the fiery arrow arching into the sky and he urged his men on. "We must hurry," he said. "A brave fighter needs our help."

The King and his men galloped hard and fast until, at nightfall, they reached the castle of the Thane of Moray. There the King asked why a burning arrow had been fired into the sky. The Thane told him that it had been the signal to start a rebellion, which he

120

had crushed, and the ringleader was to be executed the following morning.

When the King enquired as to how he could help kill the Island Beast, the Thane said that he himself had slain it with his own sword. He entertained the King with a magnificent feast and told him many lies about how well he treated the people of Moray.

But this King was a clever King. In addition to listening to the Thane, he listened to what others were saying. He heard the servants speaking in the hall and the cooks conversing in the kitchen. He heard the maids murmuring in the pantry and the grooms gossiping in the stables.

This clever King looked at the face of the Thane and saw greed and cruelty.

He looked at the faces of the people and their children and he saw fear and hunger.

When morning came and the Boy was led out to be executed, the King raised his hand.

"Stop!" he ordered. "I would hear a plea from the accused."

The Boy told his story plainly. Of how the people paid taxes that they could not afford. Of how they were obliged to give a portion of their livestock and their crops to the Thane so that there was not enough for themselves. Of how they had to feed what they had left to the Island Beast. Of how the Thane had sent the villagers to slay the Beast with no help from him or his men.

The Thane declared the Boy's story to be false.

An argument arose and the King summoned the youngest child who could speak, "For," he said, "from the mouths of little ones comes forth the truth."

But, being a clever King, he had also sent a trusted advisor to search the island on Loch Loy. This man reported that the Island Beast had been slain with a blazing arrow shot down its throat to pierce its heart, and not by the sword of the Thane.

The youngest child spoke clearly to the King of how the villagers lived and how they fed the Island Beast each week. He told of how the Thane had come to visit them when they could not pay their taxes in cattle and in kind. And how the Thane would not send his men to fight the Beast, but had made the Boy go to the island with his bow and only one arrow. The Boy had slain the Island Beast, and now the Thane intended to kill the Boy.

The King cast the Thane into the deepest dungeon and he ordered the Boy to be released and brought before him.

"Boy of no name," said the King, "I will bestow a name upon you. From this day forth you will be called '*Brogach*' or 'Brodie', which means 'sturdy lad'. You will be chief of a new clan, and the symbol of this clan will be a hand clutching arrows in its fist."

Thus the Boy became Brodie, chief of his own clan, and he wore a crest of a hand clutching arrows in its fist. And Brodie lived long, to rule his people both wisely and well.

Wood kindling burning on a fire

Snow and snow and more snow

All I can tell you is what I know

the everlasting snow that rests there

Nostrils quivering, it sniffed the air

The Big Grey Man
of Ben Macdui

All over the world there are stories about haunted mountains, tales of Bigfoot or the Yeti: huge two-footed creatures – part man, part mythical beast – who appear, to menace or give warning to travellers. Known in earlier times as 'Greymen' in Scotland, it is only in the last century that stories began to circulate of one such creature roaming the summit and passes of Ben Macdui, the highest peak of the Cairngorms.

Some climbers say the Big Grey Man is only a Brocken spectre – an effect that occurs when the sun reflects your own shadow into low cloud, making a great shadowy shape appear.

Read the story and decide for yourself.

125

This is a tale so tall, so strange, and so mysterious, that I am not sure I believe it myself.

At the beginning of winter I was travelling over the Cairngorms, a massive and majestic mountain range in the Highlands of Scotland. The track I followed had already felt the icy winds of the north and was partly covered by early snowfall. Some people dislike being among the hills. In particular they avoid the area around Ben Macdui, finding it to be eerie and oppressive. But I scoffed at their stories of a great grey man-creature roaming those slopes.

Striding through the pass that day, I happily breathed the clear air of the mountain. The topmost peaks were heavy with the everlasting snow that rests there, but the sun was shining, and I sang as I marched along. Far from being alone on my journey, I had the best of company. A flash of red let me know that deer were grazing in the distance. I spotted a brace of ptarmigan, moulting their summer coat into white to blend with the backdrop, and so hopefully survive another season in this disguise. And in the heavens soared the golden eagle, master of the skies.

126

I was not interested in hunting any of these. My haversack held plenty of food and drink and my stomach was full with a good breakfast.

Fresh snow started to fall. This did not worry me. I was wearing heavy trousers, jumper, jacket, hat and sturdy boots. The staff I carried was stout and my warm plaid was wrapped snug about me. Besides which, I had my emergency whistle strung around my neck – when I am hiking I never take this off. It's there to signal my location and summon help if I have an accident.

I kept climbing the track that would take me to the other side of Ben Macdui and the place where I intended to rest at nightfall. The atmosphere was calm, the mountain still and beautiful. But there is always danger in the Scottish hills. Winter is when weather changes are swift, and occasionally deadly.

Without warning the snow thickened to a blizzard. Onwards I trudged. Too far into the journey to turn back, I was confident to continue, for soon I would begin my descent. Half an hour later I was weary, as if I had walked for hours. The snow stopped falling. I paused to drink from my bottle and it was then that I first felt I was not alone.

Mist came swirling at my feet, and then creeping, creeping, creeping, higher and higher, until it enveloped my waist, my shoulders, and finally my head. There were shapes among the swirls and eddies of the mist. They shifted. Drifting here… Drifting there…

There!

A definite form. I blinked. It was gone.

"Enough," I told myself, "time to be on your way." Throwing off my uneasiness I shouldered my haversack to set forth again.

"Aiee!" I screamed.

Directly in front of me loomed a huge beast with black eyes and an array of spiky horns protruding from the top of its head.

I gasped. It was a stag – a monarch of the glen – bearing magnificent antlers. It pawed the ground. I must have wandered astray and blundered into a herd of hinds and fawns. Stags do not take kindly to intruders. They defend their territory violently. In an attempt

to show I was no threat,
I remained motionless. But
the stag was not convinced. It
lowered its antlers to charge at me.
I was sore afraid. In a match between
us, I was the weaker; I would have to
be nimble to avoid being gored.

Then the stag hesitated and raised
its head. Nostrils quivering, it sniffed
the air, eyes wide and startled. I saw it
tremble in fear as it stared beyond me.
Its whole body shuddered and it sprang.
Not towards me in battle, but bounding
away, running for its life.

I turned. Behind me the mist had
gathered more densely. But in it, for the
briefest second, I saw a shape. What it
was I could not say. But it was immense,
much bigger than the stag. What animal
was larger than a full-grown stag? My heart
thudded in my chest. No natural creature that
I could think of.

"Who is there?" my voice quavered as I asked the question.

No answer.

"Will you show yourself to me?" I asked.

No answer.

"We could walk together," I suggested.

No answer.

With unsteady hands I gripped my staff and went on. I had scarce gone seven paces when I was aware of steps crunching through the snow. The footfall of something behind me – a firmer, deeper tread than my own.

I whirled round. Within the shadows I discerned a human shape. Well, almost human, but much wider and taller, with a hairy head and long arms trailing along the ground. I strove to dispel the fear flooding my mind. If I were to be killed I would at least see whatever stalked me.

I made a step forward. It moved back.

Another step by me. Again, it moved back.

For each step I made, it moved back.

I realised that I would not get near to it. Every step it took was worth three of mine. I was merely wasting my energy. But I was sick of being frightened.

"Get thee gone from here!" I yelled. "Depart and annoy me no more!" Shaking my staff, I stamped my booted feet on the ground and made a show of fierceness.

The mist cleared and it was gone.

It's easy to take a wrong turn when trekking in the hills. I stumbled on, but the track was lost to me. I was sensible enough to keep heading in the right direction but I was no longer on a safe route for walkers. The sun was out again. Sun shining on fresh snow makes the mountainside unstable. I walked faster.

Suddenly, cracking like a whiplash, came the sound every mountaineer dreads. An avalanche! I glanced up. Roaring down the mountain was an enormous mass of snow. And I was in its path!

Within seconds I was caught up in the choking tumble. Snow in my hair and eyelashes, filling my nose and mouth. I struggled to bind my face with my plaid and curled up as the full force of the crashing snow struck me. The avalanche rolled me over and over and over down the mountainside. When it eventually halted, I lay buried underneath.

I had no clue whether I was upside down or back to front. Flailing my arms I made a space in which to breathe. I knew I had but minutes to escape this trap. I grabbed a handful of snow, compressed it into a small ball, and flung it from me. Watching how it fell I could tell which way was up and which way was down. With my bare hands I dug a tunnel and thrust my head into the air.

Snow and snow and more snow. Above and about me, for miles and miles. I wormed out and dragged myself free.

My plaid, my staff, my haversack, all were gone. Only my whistle remained round my neck. I floundered, waist deep in a sea of whiteness, utterly exhausted. In despair, for I believed that I was going to die, I put my whistle to my lips and gave a feeble blow. My last desperate cry for help. Then I sank into a stupor.

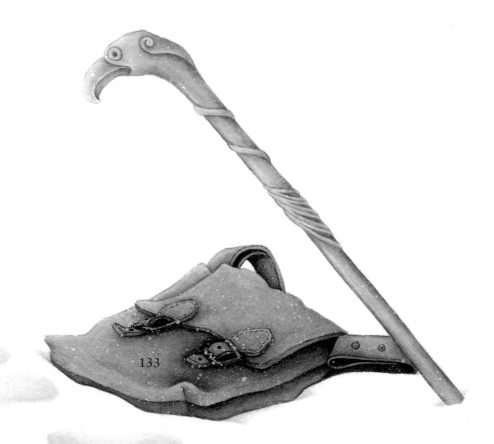

133

I awoke to a crackling sound. Wood kindling burning on a fire. I felt the warmth of it near my face. I lifted my head and opened my eyes.

I could not see.

I rubbed my eyes and prodded at my eyelids but to no avail. Although my eyes were wide open there was no sight within them. I was suffering from snow blindness. Where was I? I could hear a storm raging yet the wind was not near me.

"Hello!" I called. By the echo I guessed that I was in a cave. I tried to sit up but I was too weak. "Is there anyone there?"

A low grunt in my ear. Then a hairy hand, sized more like a paw, supported me, and a vessel – by the feel of it, a clay pot – was held to my mouth.

I supped hot broth and fell back to sleep: the fevered sleep of the delirious. I know not what time passed. Later I judged that I had sheltered in the cave for three days. For those days and nights I was as weak as a kitten. I woke, I ate, I slept, protected from the elements by rough blankets over me and a mattress of straw below me. And tended by a being I could not see.

"Who are you?" I ventured once.

There was no answer. But there was no need for an answer. I knew the name of my rescuer. He was the Big Grey Man of Ben Macdui. Pondering on my situation I realised that he had begun to follow me when I had strayed from the track. I deduced that he summoned the mist to conceal me from the stag and, when that

failed, frightened it off, as it might have killed me. He had tried to protect me because he knew I was lost. The shrill note of the whistle had alerted him to my plight and he had brought me to this cave after the avalanche.

"I would like to thank you," I told him when I began to feel better.

The Big Grey Man of Ben Macdui growled softly.

"Is there anything I could give you as a token of my gratitude?" I asked.

There was a silence. I believe the creature was thinking.

Then a rustling.

Hot breath close to my face.

The hairs on my neck rose up. The Big Grey Man of Ben Macdui was going to eat me! He had been feeding me and caring for me to make me a tastier meal!

Long fingers fumbled at my neck.

I quaked in terror.

The Big Grey Man of Ben Macdui lifted the string of my emergency whistle. Then a hairy paw placed the whistle into my palm.

"Ah!" I sobbed in relief as I understood what he wanted. Removing the whistle from round my neck, I held it up. Blindly waving my hands in a flourish, I made a gesture of presenting it to my saviour.

The Big Grey Man of Ben Macdui gave a happy grunt and patted the top of my head.

During that night my sleep was disturbed. I opened my eyes. Something was different. The wind had stopped. Dawn light was breaking at the entrance to the cave.

Glory be! The storm was over.

I sat up. Dawn! Light! I could see again!

Happiness swept through me. I slept once more and enjoyed the sweetest rest I'd had for days.

It was late morning before I awoke properly. Sunlight was pouring into the cave. In trepidation I raised my head to face the Big Grey Man of Ben Macdui.

But he was nowhere to be seen. Apart from my presence, the cave was completely empty.

Whenever I recount this story I can see the reaction of those who listen. They doubt my words, much as you are doing now. You think I imagined what happened to me. Due to fatigue and snow blindness I experienced hallucinations. The shape in the mist was an optical illusion. Sunlight in the clouds created the impression of a great grey man.

All I can tell you is what I know.

I searched the cave. There was no trace of the presence of the Big Grey Man of Ben Macdui. There was no clay pot, no blankets, no straw mattress.

Neither was there a whistle around my neck.

not the footprints of a man nor woman

the wind raged outside

Must never be seen

the body of a man but the head and paws of a wolf

Wulver is Wulver

The Wulver

Scotland's most northerly isles, the Shetland Islands, are home to the beautiful stocky Shetland ponies.

They are also the home of the Wulver – a mythical creature who has the body of a man but the head, feet and hands of a wolf. Tradition tells us that the Wulver is kind and helpful, and gives away the fish he catches.

Early every morning, Jarita and Jarl rose from their beds to help their parents prepare for work.

They helped their father arrange his nets in his boat, and waved him goodbye as he sailed out into deep water to harvest the fish that the family needed to live. They helped their mother strap on a long wicker creel, and waved her goodbye as she set off to sell yesterday's catch at the farmhouses inland. Then Jarl and Jarita would go to the field beside their cottage to harness up their pony.

They called this pony 'Sheltie', for she was a true Shetland pony of the broad and sturdy kind, bred only on those islands which lie in the wild waters of the Atlantic Ocean far north of Scotland. Sheltie stood no higher than an eight-year-old child, had a chestnut-brown coat, a silky white mane, and dark eyes with long black eyelashes.

"You are the most beautiful Shetland pony in all the Shetland Islands," Jarita would whisper in the pony's ear.

"And you are the strongest pony in all the Shetland Islands," Jarl would say as he clambered onto her back.

Then Jarita would climb up behind her big brother and they would ride off to the village school along a track overlooking the cliffs.

It happened one morning that the wind was blowing hard, as it often does on the Shetland Islands, and the water was roiling and boiling around the cliffs.

Jarita shaded her eyes and looked towards the horizon. "I hope Daddy doesn't get caught in a storm at sea."

"Our daddy can read the weather," said Jarl. "He has fished the seas for many years and knows its every mood."

When Jarita and Jarl reached the village they tethered their pony with a long rope and left her to graze on the scattald beside the schoolhouse. Through lesson time and lunch time the wind raged outside. It tugged at the chimney pots and rattled the windows, but the schoolhouse was solid and stood firm against the bluster.

After school they mounted their pony to make their way home. Jarita put her arms around her brother and hugged him tightly as they returned along the cliff track.

"The wind is getting fiercer," she said, burying her face in his jacket. "I hope that Daddy has turned his boat for home."

"Our daddy is a good sailor," Jarl reassured her.

"The ocean is so big and his boat is so small. I'm afraid that it might overturn and be lost forever."

"Our daddy will find a sheltered bay and stay there until the wind dies away."

Jarita glanced to where white foaming breakers were crashing in along the beach. She gripped her brother's arm. "What's that?" she cried in alarm.

"Where?" Jarl reined Sheltie to a halt.

Jarita pointed to something floundering about in the water.

"It's a seal," Jarl laughed, "surfing the waves as they like to do."

"No!" Jarita slid from the pony's back and went to the cliff edge. "It's not a seal."

Jarl dismounted and followed his sister. They lay down and peered over the cliff. "Indeed it is not a seal," he agreed. He watched the creature for a moment longer and then he said slowly, "But neither is it a human being."

Above the noise of the wind they could hear the creature's pitiful cries: sounds halfway between a yelp and a scream.

"Whatever it is we must rescue it," declared Jarita. "We'll take the path near here that leads to the beach."

"I'll loosen Sheltie's tether rope and bring it with us," Jarl called after his sister as she began to scramble down the cliff path. "Be careful!"

When Jarita reached the foot of the cliff, the storm was at full force and the sky was filled with black clouds and driving rain. Although she couldn't see very clearly, she realised that the creature was in terrible trouble. The swell of the sea was battering it back and forth and the poor thing was so weak that it could not scramble out of the water.

"Stretch out your hand!" Jarita shouted. "I will try to pull you in."

But when the creature did as she'd said, Jarita saw that it was not a hand at the end of its arm. It was a huge hairy paw.

Jarita's eyes opened wide. She waved frantically at her brother as he ran towards her carrying the rope. They stared into the gathering gloom and saw that the creature also had a huge hairy head.

"It's a wolf!" exclaimed Jarita.

"We must let it drown," Jarl said. "There are no wolves on the Shetland Islands and neither do we want there to be."

"It seems a cruel thing to do," Jarita whispered.

"A wolf would kill sheep and cattle, and even children if it got the chance."

The creature fixed pleading eyes upon the two children. "Help!" it cried out. "You, help! Please!"

The children glanced at each other. Without saying anything more, Jarl threw the tether rope into the water. The creature caught the rope and Jarl and Jarita hauled it onto the shingle beach, where it lay moaning.

It had the body of a man but the head and paws of a wolf, and was the strangest thing they had ever seen.

"We shouldn't go too close to it," Jarl warned his sister.

But, dressed in a torn shirt and trousers, its fur bedraggled and with blood oozing from a cut on its head, it didn't seem the least bit scary.

Jarita knelt down. She took her hanky out of her pocket to clean up the blood. The creature whimpered as she dabbed the wound.

"There, there," she crooned, as her mother did to her when she fell over and cut her leg or arm. "Wheesht now, you'll be bright and braw in two shakes of a lamb's tail."

They helped it sit up, and Jarl took off his jacket and wrapped it round the creature's shoulders.

"Are you a wolf?" Jarl asked.

Although they'd never heard of there being wolves on the Shetland Islands, the children had seen pictures of them in story books.

"No. I am not wolf," the creature replied in a gruff voice.

"What are you, then?" asked Jarita.

"I am Wulver," the creature replied.

"We've never met a Wulver before," said Jarl.

"And I have never spoken to one of you small creatures before," said the Wulver. "But I am very glad today is the day that I did."

"So are we." Jarita smiled.

The Wulver studied her face carefully and copied her smile in return. But the Wulver had an *awful* lot of sharp-looking teeth, so his smile didn't appear as friendly as he might have imagined.

"What is a Wulver?" Jarita asked.

The Wulver gave her a puzzled look. "Wulver," he said, "is Wulver."

"Do you have a name?" said Jarl.

"Wulver."

"Jarl is asking about your given name," Jarita explained. "What should we call you?"

"You call me 'Wulver', for that is what I am."

"My name is Jarl," said Jarl. "It means 'an earl'."

"My name is Jarita," said Jarita. "It means 'a bird'."

"My name is Wulver," said the Wulver. "It means 'Wulver'."

Jarita giggled.

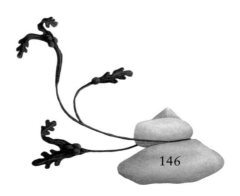

146

"How did you fall into the sea?" she asked Wulver.

"Hit head on rock. Big wave knock me in water when I am fishing. There." The Wulver pointed to a huge rock that stood in the water a few yards offshore. "My fishing rock. My Wulver Stane."

"Why have we never seen you before?"

"Wulver always fish on seaward side. Hide when boats pass. Must never be seen."

"Where do you live?"

"In cave."

Jarl and Jarita helped Wulver stumble up to his cave, which was in the cliff above the high-tide water line.

Wulver's home was snug, lined with blankets and filled with oddments he must have collected on the beach at low tide. Jarl and Jarita, who'd often gone beachcombing themselves, knew that lots of interesting things floated in from the huge ships that passed on their way to the Americas on the far side of the world.

"You have a lovely home," Jarl said politely.

"Yes," said Wulver. "But now Wulver must go somewhere else."

"Please don't go somewhere else," said Jarita, disappointed. She'd been looking forward to telling everyone in school next day of how she had rescued Wulver from the sea. She'd hoped she might see him again and perhaps bring him some scones she'd baked herself.

"We could visit you and you could visit us," said Jarl. "We'd like to be your friend."

Wulver shook his big head.

"That is why I must move," he said. "We can never be friends."

"Why not?" Jarita protested.

"Once people see Wulver they shout and throw stones. Chase Wulver with swords and pitchforks."

"Please stay," said Jarl. "We won't tell anyone about you."

"Yes, you will." Wulver looked at the children with wisdom in his eyes. "Wulver stay one day more. Then Wulver find new cave. You will not see Wulver again. But Wulver thanks you for his life."

When Jarita and Jarl eventually reached home, their mother was standing at the door of the cottage.

"Where have you been?" she called out to them. But before they could reply, she went on: "Your father had an accident as he tried to reach safe harbour in the storm. The boat ran on to a rock and his arm is broken."

Jarita screamed and jumped down from the pony.

"Don't worry, my dearie," her mother hugged her. "Your daddy is quite alright and sitting by the fire. But it will be weeks before the boat is repaired and his arm healed enough for him to go out to fish."

Jarl and Jarita knew this was a disaster. It was selling fish that fed and clothed them and gave them boots to wear in winter.

"It is indeed a bleak day for this house." Their mother took the savings jar from the mantelpiece and emptied the money onto the kitchen table. When she'd counted it she exchanged a look with their father and said, "There is not enough here to see us through the days and weeks ahead. We must think on how we might manage to put food on our table."

That night after the family had eaten their evening meal, Jarl and Jarita's mother and father spoke to them.

"There are difficult decisions to be made in our house. We must be brave and our two children must be especially brave."

Jarl spoke up, "I will help repair the boat and, if it is seaworthy before Daddy's arm is healed, then I will take it out and fish the seas."

"My son," his mother replied, "you are yet too young to handle the boat and the net."

Jarita spoke up, "I will cast the net and help draw it in."

"My daughter," her father replied, "you are yet too small to cast the net and draw it in."

"We will do it together," said Jarl and Jarita.

Jarl and Jarita's parents shook their heads. "We will not place our children in such danger."

"Then how can we eat?" asked Jarita.

"How can we live?" asked Jarl.

"You are being called to do a braver thing than go out in your daddy's boat," their mother replied, and tears dropped from her eyes as she spoke.

"Tomorrow will be the last time that Sheltie can carry you to and from school," said their father. "After that you must walk the road yourselves, there and back again."

"I do not mind walking the long road to school and back again each day," said Jarita.

"Nor do I," said Jarl. "But what will Sheltie do when we are at school?"

Their father spoke with sorrow in his voice. "Tomorrow's morrow I will take Sheltie to be sold. The price she brings us will see us through until I am well enough to repair our boat and fish the seas again."

Jarita wept as she lay in bed that night and Jarl brushed his own tears away while he comforted his sister.

The next day Jarl and Jarita did not chat with each other like they usually did when Sheltie carried them to school. On the way home on the cliff path Jarita suddenly burst out: "This will be the very last time we will ever ride our pony, Sheltie! My heart is breaking with sadness."

"Mine too," said her brother. "But Sheltie must be sold, for father cannot fish the sea with a broken arm."

Unknown to the children, in his cave below, the Wulver listened to what they were saying.

That night, as she would have no fish to sell the next day, nor for many a day after, their mother put the empty creel outside the door of their cottage.

But the next morning, when Jarl and Jarita opened the door to walk to school, the creel was brimming over with fish. To the children's great joy they were allowed to keep Sheltie for another day.

Every day after that, the same thing happened. At night the empty creel was left outside and in the morning it was full of fish.

"Our friends and neighbours must be sharing their catch with us," said the children's mother.

"Indeed they must," the children's father agreed, "for how else would our creel be filled with fish each morning?"

Jarita and Jarl said nothing at all.

One day when winter came and their mother went outside to strap on the fish creel, she saw prints in the snow. They were not footprints of man nor woman, but of something else entirely.

"Gracious me!" she said. "It is a wonder our fish have not been eaten for there was some creature prowling round our door last night." She examined the tracks in the snow. "If I didn't know better I might think it to be a wolf."

"It's not a wolf track," said Jarita.

"It's a Wulver," said Jarl before he could stop himself.

"Whatever is a Wulver?" asked their mother.

To which the children replied, "Wulver is Wulver."

"That's a good name for a made-up friend," their mother laughed. "I'll be glad anyway that, from tomorrow, we'll need no more charity. Your father is fit and well enough to go fishing again."

On the way to school that morning, Jarl and Jarita brought their beloved pony Sheltie to a halt near the cliff path that led to the beach.

"Daddy is better now!" Jarita called out as loudly as she could.

Jarl cupped his hands to his mouth: "We do not need your help any more."

Then both children shouted: "Thank you very much, Wulver."

From the cliffs an echo came back: *Wulver... Wulver... Wulver...*

Although Jarita and Jarl searched the cliff face for many a day and more, they never found Wulver's new cave home. And though they scanned every large rock in the sea, they never saw Wulver fishing on his new Wulver Stane.

But now and then, when walking on the beach, they would come across the print of a large paw in the sand.

slice the peat into thick slabs

the little sprite in the smart green coat and bright red leggings

ablaze with the light of many lanterns

twenty days and nights of this dancing and sleeping passed

The Wee Folk of Merlin Crag

In Lanarkshire there is a peat bog with an upraised section of ground known as a crag. It was long believed that Merlin the Wizard put a door there which led into the Other World.

The peat cutters who worked in the bog would always avoid that area for they knew that it would be foolish to disturb the fairies or 'Wee Folk' who lived inside the crag.

A long time ago in the county of Lanark

a poor peat cutter called Dougal lived with his wife and children in a lowly hut on the edge of a moor.

Dougal's job was to gather peat from the moss bogs that his master owned. The moorland was mainly flat – apart from one rocky outcrop. This was known as Merlin Crag and believed by some to belong to the Other People. Out of respect for these Wee Folk, Dougal always avoided this hill and confined himself to working in the surrounding peat banks.

Firstly, Dougal would dig down a few inches and remove the top mossy layer of earth. Putting that turf to one side, he'd cut deep into the wet brown peat with his slane spade, which is curved, much like a shinty stick. Then he would slice the peat into thick slabs and turn each piece to expose it to the sun and the wind.

When the slabs dried out he'd stack them upright until he was ready to carry them to the master's barn. From morning dawn until evening dusk, Dougal toiled, rarely resting from his labours.

One day, when Dougal had taken all the peat from the bog where he was working, he decided to have a short break. It was dinner time, so he ate the food he had brought with him. After he'd finished his meal he stretched his muscles to ease his aching back and arms.

At that moment, the master, who was riding past on his horse, caught sight of Dougal. This master was a loud-mouthed bully who seldom listened to what others had to say. *Oho!* he thought. *There's a man resting instead of labouring. I'd better deal with him.*

"Hey you!" the master shouted at Dougal. "I don't pay you to stand around doing nothing."

"I have been working hard," Dougal replied. "I only left off for a moment to have a drink of water and a bite to eat."

"Keep on working, you lazy man!" the master shouted louder.

"I've cut the peat from this bog so I'll move on to another," said Dougal, and he picked up his spades.

"Get along with you!" the master shouted even louder. He pointed to the crag that overlooked the bog. "Why have you not cut peat from up there?"

"That's the Crag of Merlin," said Dougal, "and well kent as the place of the Wee Folk. It would be wise not to disturb their ground."

"Nonsense!" the master shouted in his loudest voice. "I order you to dig out peat from the top of that hill."

"I beg you to reconsider," Dougal protested.

But the master would not heed his pleas. "You will do what I say," he ordered, "else I will not pay your wages. You will be forced to leave your home and wander the road, with no money to feed and clothe your wife and children."

"The Wee Folk have lived there since the time of the wizard Merlin, and before and beyond that," said Dougal.

"Well I live here now," snapped the master. "I own this land and will do with it as I please."

"No good can come of this," Dougal muttered to himself while he reluctantly climbed the hill to Merlin Crag.

The sun was beginning to set as Dougal raised his spade and struck his first blow into the heathery top of Merlin Crag.

A sudden shriek sounded through the air.

Dougal paused and looked about him. Shadows were seeping over the moorland, but he could see no one. He returned to his task and eased his slane spade under a great sod of turf.

A sharp scream sounded through the air.

Again, Dougal paused and looked about him. He scratched his head in puzzlement. Across the wide moor there was no sign of a human creature. Dougal resumed his task and tugged at the turf to loosen it.

A sudden shriek *and* a sharp scream sounded through the air. Dougal jumped in surprise when a little sprite, no bigger than the size of a slab of peat, appeared on the handle of his slane. It wore a smart green coat over bright red leggings, and had a tiny pointed hat perched upon its head.

"Stop!" it screeched at Dougal. "Whatever it is you are doing, stop it immediately!"

"I am cutting peat, as I have been told to," said Dougal.

"You are pulling the roof off my house," said the little sprite. "If I have no roof on my house then the rain, and the hail, and the snow, and the wild winter wind will blow me and my furniture and my dishes here, there and everywhere."

Dougal knelt down to speak to the little creature. "I am very sorry," he said. "I did not intend to pull the roof off your house. I do not want the rain, and the hail, and the snow, and the wild winter wind to blow you and your furniture and your dishes here, there and everywhere."

"I am glad to hear that," said the little sprite. "Go away and don't come back to annoy me."

"That I cannot do." And Dougal, who was a gentle soul, began to weep in pity for the little creature. "I must keep working in this place," he sobbed. "If I do not cut this peat my master will not pay me. I will be forced to leave my home and wander the road, with no money to feed and clothe my wife and children."

"I'm sure that if you explain the situation to your master he will understand," the little sprite told Dougal. "No man of common decency would destroy another living being's home."

Dougal doubted that his master possessed the common decency that the little sprite accorded him. The master had never shown himself to be a good and generous man. But Dougal agreed that he would go and explain to his master that taking peat from Merlin Crag would destroy the home of the little sprite.

When Dougal arrived at the master's house it was ablaze with the light of many lanterns. The master was entertaining and had laid out a lavish feast, with as much food and drink on the dining table as Dougal and his family ate in a year and a day.

"I have never heard such a silly story!" the master scoffed as Dougal told his tale. "You are an idle good-for-nothing fellow, who is trying to avoid doing a full day's work."

"Nay," said Dougal, "but I'm agin turning anybody out of their home. And also, I am afeard what will happen if we disturb the Wee Folk."

"Well, I am not afeard of anything," the master boasted. "I will go directly to where you were working, and, if I meet any of these Wee Folk, you may have Merlin Crag to keep for yourself."

His guests laughed uproariously and so, to entertain them more, the master added, "Indeed, if a little sprite appears and speaks to me then I declare that my peat cutter, Dougal, may have all the land I own and my house too for that matter."

Witnessed by all present, the master wrote out a deed of land rights for Dougal and he signed it and stuck the paper in the front window of his house. Then the whole party, holding lanterns aloft, trooped along the road to Merlin Crag.

The master's friends watched while he went up onto the crag and, with his two hands, seized a clod of earth and hauled on it.

A sudden shriek sounded through the air.

The master kept pulling at the turf.

A sharp scream sounded through the air.

Still the master went on pulling at the turf.

A sudden shriek *and* a sharp scream sounded through the air. A little sprite, no bigger than the size of a slab of peat, appeared. It wore a smart green coat over bright red leggings, and had a tiny pointed hat perched upon its head.

"Stop!" it screeched at the master. "Whatever it is you are doing, stop it immediately!"

"I will not stop," the master replied, "for I am entitled to take peat from my own bog."

"You are pulling the roof off my house," said the little sprite. "If I have no roof on my house then the rain, and the hail, and the snow, and the wild winter wind will blow me and my furniture and my dishes here, there and everywhere."

The master knelt down to speak to the little creature. "I am not in the least sorry," he shouted. "I do not care if I pull the roof off your house. I do not care if the rain, and the hail, and the snow, and the wild winter wind blow you and your furniture and your dishes here, there and everywhere."

Hearing these words, the little sprite stamped its foot upon the earth. There was a peal of thunder and a flash of lightning. A magic door in the rocks crashed open and out streamed a multitude of the Wee Folk. They leapt on the master, scrambling up his legs and arms, pinching and nipping as they went.

"Oh, no! Oh, no!" The master hopped from one foot to the other. "No! No! No!" He swatted at them, but they reached his shoulders and his face where they scratched at his ears and nose and tore at his hair.

The master fell upon the ground and the Wee Folk rolled him over and over and over, through the magic door, and it shut fast behind them.

Inside the Crag of Merlin the Wee Folk fastened the master to a post with a thread around his wrist. Although the thread was made of gossamer he could not break it, no matter how hard he tried. The Wee Folk fed the master and bade him drink their heather brew. Afterwards they prodded him with sticks to make him dance for their amusement.

The master drank and danced until he was weary, whereupon he lay down to sleep. When he awoke he begged to be set free, but the little sprite in the smart green coat and bright red leggings with the tiny pointed hat perched upon its head said, "The time has not yet come for you to leave us."

Again the master drank and danced until he was weary and laid himself down to sleep. Again, when he awoke he begged to be set free, but the little sprite in the smart green coat and bright red leggings with the tiny pointed hat perched upon its head said, "The time has not yet come for you to leave us."

By dint of counting on his fingers and toes, the master reckoned that twenty days and nights of this dancing and sleeping passed. When he awoke on the twentieth day and begged for the twentieth time to be set free, the little sprite in the smart green coat and bright red leggings with the tiny pointed hat perched upon its

head said, "The time has come for you to leave us, for the turf that you dislodged has grown back over my house."

On saying these words the little sprite stamped its foot upon the earth. There was a peal of thunder and a flash of lightning and the magic door crashed open. As fast as he was able, the master ran through it, and it shut fast behind him.

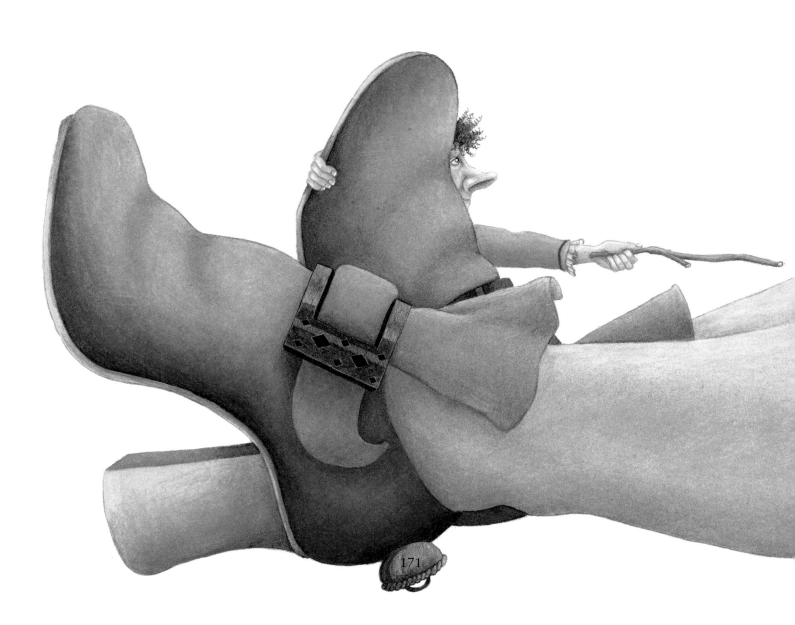

The master ran and ran and ran until he came to his own house. There were children playing happily in the garden and an old man sat by the door.

The master asked the old man, "Who are you?"

The old man replied, "I am the master of this house."

"That cannot be," said the master, "for I am the master of this house. Twenty days ago I went to Merlin Crag to prove to my peat cutter, Dougal, that there was no such thing as Wee Folk."

"Twenty days ago!" came the reply. "That happened twenty years ago."

"Oh, no!" said the master. "A trick was played on me and I was kept prisoner in a hidden cave. But I counted the days and nights on my fingers and toes and only twenty days have passed."

"Twenty years have been and gone since you went to Merlin Crag and disturbed the ground of the Wee Folk," said the old man. "I know this for a fact, as I am Dougal, the peat cutter, and these are my children's children playing happily in the garden."

"This cannot be," said the master, "for I have not become older in any way."

"That is because you have been living with the Wee Folk," Dougal told him, "while I and my family have lived in this house. You signed a deed giving your land and house to me if you met the Wee Folk, so I now own this house and the land around it."

The master looked and saw that the deed he had signed was still stuck in the front window of his house. It was brown and crinkled with age. And he looked again at the old man and saw that he was indeed the peat cutter called Dougal.

"What am I to do?" he lamented. "With neither home nor land, I will be forced to wander the road with no money to feed and clothe myself."

"I will allow you to dwell in my hut on the edge of the moor," said Dougal, "and I will give you a job working on the moss bogs. But there is one condition attached to this."

"What is your condition?" the master asked him.

"You must promise me," said Dougal, "that you will never cut peat from the top of Merlin Crag."

173

revenge is going to taste delicious

she honked loudly and flapped her wings

chunk of homemade cheese shone in the sun

Some hae meat and canna eat

a flurry of feathers

The Saving Grace

Here is Mr Fox up to his old tricks in a story based on the traditional tale 'The Fox and the Goose', but with a twist at the end…

There was once a girl called Kirsty MacLeod.

She was just an ordinary girl, who lived in an ordinary house with ordinary parents. Kirsty had long red hair and every morning Kirsty's father would brush out Kirsty's long red hair and Kirsty's mother would pleat it into one single plait that hung down her back.

One of Kirsty's tasks on the farm where they lived was to feed and water Griselda, the family goose. It was very important that Kirsty looked after the goose, because Griselda was better than a watchdog on the farm. If she sensed danger she honked loudly and flapped her wings. And anytime she saw the wily fox prowling about the henhouse or creeping up on the baby ducklings, Griselda ran at him, hissing, with her neck outstretched, to chase him away.

Kirsty loved Griselda and fed her regularly, making sure she had clean water every day. Now and then Kirsty would take the goose for a stroll along the riverbank because she knew that Griselda especially loved to drink fresh river water.

There were bushes by the river and one day, when Kirsty was walking with Griselda, the wily fox decided to sneak in among these bushes.

"Aha!" he said to himself. "I will hide in here and spy on that fine fat goose. No more will she stop me stealing chickens from the henhouse. No more will she spoil my fun when I try to catch the fluffy little ducklings. Today, I will catch her instead. She may be slick and quick in the farmyard, but out here in the wide world *I* am the master."

So the wily fox watched and waited, and he waited and watched. And, soon enough, Griselda came waddling towards him.

"My revenge is going to taste delicious," the wily fox laughed, and he smacked his lips together.

Then the wily fox noticed Kirsty following on behind the goose.

"Oh no!" he said. "This might be harder than I thought. I will have to wait until that little girl is not beside the goose before I make my move."

The wily fox remembered he had met Kirsty before while crossing a bridge over this same river. On that occasion she had caused him to bite off his own tail! He looked around at his lovely long red tail, which had since grown in, and he thought, *I may have been tripped up once, but I'm all the smarter for it. I will have this goose to eat, as I will not let this little girl trick me again.*

Kirsty was hungry and decided it was time to have her midday meal of fresh bread and salty cheese. She opened up the cloth in which these were wrapped and laid it on a patch of grass.

The smell of warm bread wafted through the air. The chunk of homemade cheese shone in the sun.

"Mmmm," said Kirsty. "I can mind my goose while I sit here in the sunshine."

The wily fox kept his eyes on the goose, who had wandered to the edge of the water. He crept closer and closer to his prey. Griselda stretched her neck to take a drink.

The wily fox pounced.

There was a snarl and a cry. A flurry of feathers. A splatter and spray of water. The jaws of the wily fox snapped shut. Poor Griselda beat her wings; she twisted this way and that.

But the wily fox had a firm grip of the goose between his teeth.

"Let go of Griselda!" Kirsty shouted. She picked up a long stick and began to beat the wily fox about the body. "Let go my goose!"

But the wily fox would not let go.

The more Kirsty shrieked and hit him with her stick, the more tightly the wily fox held on to the goose. Kirsty saw that she must stop or the wily fox would bite harder and then he would surely kill Griselda.

Kirsty suddenly recalled a previous meeting she'd had with this creature on the river bridge. She realised that she would have to think carefully how best to deal with the wily fox if she was to save her pet goose.

"All right then, you may have my goose. And welcome to it, that's what I say." Kirsty swung her long red plait over her shoulder and went and flopped upon the grass. "I will eat my dinner and you may eat yours. And, if you wish, we can sit together and enjoy the view."

The wily fox looked at Kirsty. Kirsty waved to him in a friendly manner and picked up a chunk of bread.

And the wily fox thought, *I do believe I might have the goose* and *the cheese* and *the warm bread, and perhaps eat that little girl also, if I am so minded*. He was so taken by this idea that he came nearer to where Kirsty sat. And she smiled and spoke to him in a soft voice.

"I am sure you behave politely when you join someone for a meal," she said. "I would expect no less from such an obviously intelligent animal."

The wily fox nodded. He considered himself an *exceptionally* intelligent animal. After all, stories of clever foxes were told in tales the whole world over. Wasn't one of the best-known sayings 'as cunning as a fox'? And did not the fox, in song and story, always get the better of his opponent?

The wily fox was now only a step away.

Kirsty's smile became wider. "I trust you to be a good dinner companion."

Oh do, please trust me, foolish little girl, thought the wily fox. *It will make the eating of you even easier than I'd hoped.* He sat down opposite Kirsty, where he could reach to grab her when he'd finished off the goose.

"And being so clever, you will have the same table manners as myself," Kirsty went on. "It would surprise me if you could not do as I do before eating. Are you able to recite our traditional Scottish grace before meals as well as I can?"

Of course I am able to recite our Scottish grace! thought the wily fox. *Better than you could recite it, on any day of the week. Indeed I know the verse off by heart.*

Some hae meat and canna eat,
And some hae nane that want it,
But I hae meat and I can eat,
And so I say – be thankit!

And the wily fox, thinking he would not be bested by a mere child, opened his mouth to say the words.

Thereupon Kirsty leaned across and whacked him on the head with her stick. Griselda saw her chance, and gave him a sharp peck on the nose. Then she wriggled free and flew up into the air.

The fox was furious at being outwitted again. In a rage he howled at Kirsty, "You did not say the grace!"

"Why," said wily Kirsty as she ran off home with Griselda, "I have said all I am going to say to you today."

"And so have I," said Theresa Breslin.

"I have said all I am going to say in this book."

deep dark waters of Loch Ness

soft breezes caused the waves to come lap, lap, lapping on the shore

thick grass and heather of the Scottish hills

the everlasting snow that rests there

The sky darkened as an enormous winged Beast with hooked talons, glittering eyes

Glossary

A

afeard: afraid.

agin: against.

B

bana-bhuise: witch.

basalt: a dark, volcanic rock which can sometimes form vast geometric columns, as in the Giant's Causeway in Northern Ireland and Fingal's Cave in Scotland.

Bell Rock Lighthouse: an engineering triumph which was built in the early nineteenth century by Robert Stevenson. Still standing today, it is the oldest sea-washed lighthouse in the world.

Ben Macdui: the second highest mountain (after Ben Nevis) in the United Kingdom.

Benandonner: a legendary Scottish giant in Celtic mythology, who tore up the Giant's Causeway.

blarney: gossip, flattery or exaggeration.

blight: disease or pollution.

bogles: mischievous Wee Folk.

braw: good.

brazier: a small coal heater.

breacan: long plaid shawl.

Brocken spectre: a large shadow of a man on mountain clouds.

brogach/Brodie: sturdy lad. The Brodie clan of Morayshire is ancient, probably stretching back to Pictish times. Their crest shows a fist clutching arrows.

C

cailleach: old woman.

canna(e): cannot.

canny: cunning.

clootie: a cloth.

clootie dumpling: a traditional Scottish pudding made with flour, breadcrumbs, currants, suet, syrup, sugar and spices wrapped in a cloth and boiled.

coire: cauldron.

croft: a small house with a small plot of land.

corry/corrie: a circular hole like a cauldron, used to describe a concave mountainside.

Corryvreckan/*Coire Breacan*: the whirlpool in the narrow strait between the islands of Jura and Scarba.

crag: a steep, jagged rock or cliff.

creel: a large wicker basket, often used for carrying fish.

croon: to sing in a low murmur.

Cuillins: a rocky mountain range in the Isle of Skye.

D

dale: an open valley.
dell: a small wooded hollow.
dunt: a firm dull thud.

F

fiefdom: a territory controlled by a particular person.
Finn MacCool: a legendary Irish giant who, in Celtic mythology, built the Giant's Causeway.
founder: to run aground, lose direction, sink.

G

glen: a valley.
gloaming: twilight or dusk.
gossamer: very fine thread as delicate as a spider's web.
gue: in past times, a two-stringed lyre from the Shetlands.
gurly: stormy.

H

hae: have.
hamlet: a small village.
hart: a male deer.
hind: a female deer.

hither and thither: here and there.

K

ken/kent: know/known.
kin: family, relatives.
kith: friends or neighbours.

L

loch: a lake, can be inland or a sea loch.
loup: leap.

M

mull: think or ponder.

N

namby-pamby: simple and weakly sentimental.
nane: none.
nay: no.
Niseag: from Old Norse meaning a cape or a headland; the Gaelic name for the monster in Loch Ness.
Nuckelavee: a terrifying mythical Highland beast which features the gory elements of horse and human.

O

Other People: see Wee Folk
Other World: Faeryland.

P

peat: partly decomposed vegetation found in bogs and fens, used for fuel.

pitch: a dark, sticky, flammable type of tar.

plaid(ie): woven tartan cloth used as a shawl or blanket, which eventually became the modern-day kilt.

R

roiling: bubbling, churning.

S

scattald: an old Scandinavian term still used in Shetland and Orkney meaning common land used by the community for peat or pasture.

Selah: used in ancient texts to ask the reader to take note or stop and listen. 'Let those with eyes, see, and those with ears, hear.'

selkie: a mythical seal which can also assume the form of a human. *Selkie* means 'seal' in Orcadian – the language of the Orkney Islands.

Sgurr Alasdair: the highest peak of the Black Cuillin range on the Isle of Skye.

shinty: a Scottish game similar to hockey, played with a distinctive curved stick.

slane spade: a long spade used for cutting peats.

spae-wife: a wise woman or a woman who can foretell the future.

sprite: a mischievous fairy or pixie.

staff: a long stick used for support while walking.

stane: stone.

stot: to bounce or spring.

T

thane: a high-ranking Scottish lord and landowner.

thankit: thanked.

thee: you.

tumshie: an old word for turnip, and therefore an excellent insult.

W

wee: small.

Wee Folk or Other People: The names given in Scotland to the fairy folk. They were thought to dress in green when they took human form, and sometimes they tried to play tricks on humans.

wheesht: be quiet.

deep dark waters of Loch Ness

soft breezes caused the waves to come lap, lap, lapping on the shore

thick grass and heather of the Scottish hills

the everlasting snow that rests there

The sky darkened as an enormous winged Beast with hooked talons, glittering eyes

it has not kindness in its spirit, nor mercy in its mind

it snorted and stamped its feet on the shingle shore

With a tremendous judder the ship struck hard, and stuck fast.

not the footprints of a man nor woman

bind your promise with a kiss

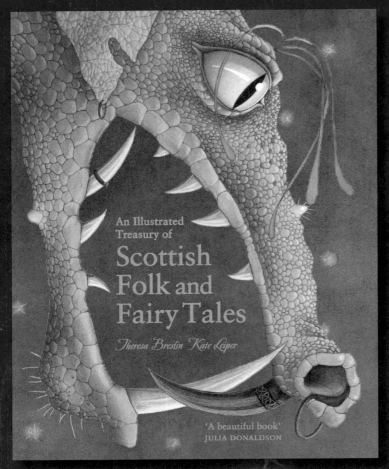
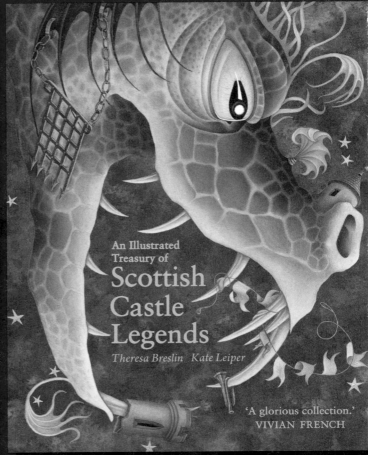